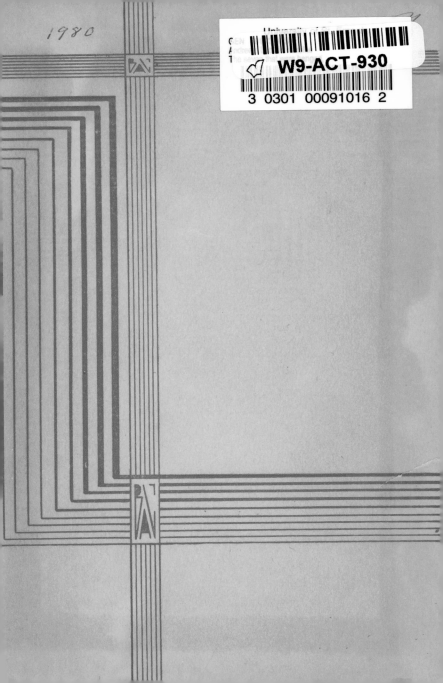

1980

THE SEVEN THAT WERE HANGED

THIS EDITION OF "THE SEVEN THAT WERE HANGED" BY LEONID ANDREYEV WAS DESIGNED, PRINTED AND BOUND EXCLUSIVELY FOR THE MEMBERS OF THE BOOK LEAGUE OF AMERICA

THE SEVEN THAT WERE HANGED

BY
LEONID ANDREYEV

NEW YORK

THE BOOK LEAGUE
OF AMERICA
MCMXXXI

THIS VOLUME CONTAINS, IN ADDITION TO "THE
SEVEN THAT WERE HANGED," ANOTHER STORY
BY ANDREYEV, CALLED "THE RED LAUGH."

MANUFACTURED BY THE H. WOLFF ESTATE
IN THE UNITED STATES OF AMERICA

The Seven that were Hanged

I

"AT ONE O'CLOCK IN THE AFTERNOON, YOUR EXCELLENCY!"

As the Minister was a very fat man, predisposed to apoplexy, and as it was necessary therefore to spare him every dangerous emotion, they took the minutest precautions in warning him that a serious attempt upon his life had been planned. When they saw that he received the news calmly, they gave him the details: the attempt was to be made the next day, at the moment when His Excellency was to leave the house to go to make his report. A few terrorists, armed with revolvers and bombs, whom a police spy had betrayed and who were now being watched by the police, were to meet near the steps at one o'clock in the afternoon, and await the Minister's exit. There the criminals would be arrested.

"Pardon me," interrupted the Minister in surprise. "How do they know that I am to go to present my report at one o'clock in the afternoon, when I learned it myself only two days ago?"

The commander of the body-guard made a vague gesture signifying ignorance.

"At one o'clock in the afternoon, Your Excellency!"

Astonished, and at the same time satisfied with the police who had managed the affair so well, the Minister shook his head; a disdainful smile appeared on his thick red lips; quickly he made all the necessary preparations to pass the night in another palace; in no way did he wish to embarrass the police. His wife and children also were removed from the dangerous premises.

As long as the lights gleamed in this new residence, and while his familiars bustled about him expressing their indignation, the Minister felt a sensation of agreeable excitement. It seemed to him that he had just received, or was about to receive, a great and unexpected reward. But the friends went away, and the lights were put out. The intermittent and fantastic glare of the arc-lights in the street fell upon the ceiling and the walls, penetrating through the high windows, symbolizing, as it were, the fragility of all bolts and walls, the vanity of all supervision. Then, in the silence and the solitude of a strange chamber, the dignitary was seized with an unspeakable terror.

He was afflicted with a kidney trouble. Every violent emotion caused his face, feet, and hands to swell, and made him appear heavier, more massive. Now, like a heap of bloated flesh that made the bed-springs bend, he suffered the anguish of the sick as he felt his face puff up and become, as it were, something foreign to his body. His thought recurred obstinately to the cruel fate that his enemies were preparing for him. He evoked one after the other all the horrible attempts of recent date, in which bombs had been thrown against persons as noble as himself and bearing even higher titles, tearing their bodies into a thousand shreds, hurling their brains against foul brick walls, and knocking their teeth from their jaws. And, at these recollections, it seemed to him that his diseased body was another man's body suffering from the fiery shock of the explosion. He pictured to himself his arms detached from his shoulders, his teeth broken, his brain crushed. His legs, stretched out in the bed, grew numb and motionless, the feet pointing upward, like those of a dead man. He breathed noisily, coughing occasionally, to avoid all resemblance to a corpse: he moved about, that he might hear the sound of the metallic springs, the rustling of the silk coverlet. And, to prove that he was really alive, he exclaimed in a loud and clear voice:

"Brave fellows! Brave fellows!"

These words of praise were for the police, the gendarmes, the soldiers, all those who protected his life and had prevented the assassination. But in vain did he stir about, lavish his praise, and smile at the discomfiture of the terrorists; he could not yet believe that he was saved. It seemed to him that the death evoked for him by the anarchists, and which existed in their thought, was already there and would remain there, refusing to go away until the assassins should be seized, deprived of their bombs, and lodged safely in prison. There it stood, in the corner yonder, declining to leave, and unable to leave, like an obedient soldier placed on guard by an unknown will.

"At one o'clock in the afternoon, Your Excellency!" This phrase came back to him continually, uttered in all tones, now joyously and ironically, now irritably, now obstinately and stupidly. One would have said that a hundred phonographs had been placed in the chamber, and were crying one after the other, with the idiotic persistence of machines:

"At one o'clock in the afternoon, Your Excellency!"

And this "one o'clock in the afternoon" of the next day, which so short a time before was in no way to be distinguished from other hours, had taken on a menacing importance; it had stepped out of the clock-dial, and was beginning to live a distinct life, stretching itself like an immense black curtain, to divide life into two parts. Before it and after it no other hour existed; it alone, presumptuous and obsessing, was entitled to a special life.

Grinding his teeth, the Minister raised himself in his bed to a sitting posture. It was positively impossible for him to sleep.

Pressing his bloated hands against his face, he pictured to himself with terrifying clearness how he would have risen on the morrow if he had been left in ignorance; he would have taken his coffee, and dressed. And neither he, or the Swiss who would have helped him on with his fur coat, or the valet who would have served his coffee, would have understood the uselessness of breakfasting and dressing, when a few moments later everything would be annihilated by the explosion. . . . The Swiss opens the door. . . . And it is he, this good and thoughtful Swiss, with the blue eyes, and the open countenance, and the numerous military decorations—he it is who opens the terrible door with his own hands. . . .

"Ah!" suddenly exclaimed the Minister aloud; slowly he removed his hands from his face. Gazing far before him into the darkness with a fixed and attentive look, he stretched out his hand to turn on the light. Then he arose, and in his bare feet walked around the strange chamber so unfamiliar to him; finding another light, he turned that on also. The room became bright and agreeable; there was only the disordered bed and the fallen coverlet to indicate a terror that had not yet completely disappeared.

Clad in a night-shirt, his beard in a tangle, a look of irritation on his face, the Minister resembled those old people who are tormented by asthma and insomnia. One would have said that the death prepared for him by others had stripped him bare, had torn him from the luxury with which he was surrounded. Without dressing he threw himself into an arm-chair, his eyes wandered to the ceiling.

"Imbeciles!" he cried in a contemptuous tone of conviction.

"Imbeciles!" And he was speaking of the policemen whom but a few moments before he had called "brave fellows," and who, through excess of zeal, had told him all the details of the attack that had been planned.

"Evidently," he thought with lucidity, "I am afraid now because I have been warned and because I know. But, if I had been left in ignorance, I should have taken my coffee quietly. And then, evidently, this death. . . . But am I then so afraid of death? I have a kidney trouble; some day I must die of it, and yet I am not afraid, because I don't know when. And these imbeciles say to me: 'At

one o'clock in the afternoon, Your Excellency!' They
thought that I would be glad to know about it! . . . Instead of that, death has placed himself in the corner yonder, and does not go away! He does not go away, because I have that fixed idea! To die is not so terrible;
the terrible thing is to know that one is going to die. It
would be quite impossible for a man to live if he knew
the hour and day of his death with absolute certainty. And
yet these idiots warn me: 'At one o'clock in the afternoon,
Your Excellency!' "

Recently he had been ill, and the doctors had told him
that he was going to die and should make his final arrange-
ments. He had refused to believe them; and, in fact, he
did not die. Once, in his youth, it had happened to him
to get beyond his depth; he had decided to put an end to
his existence; he had loaded his revolver, written some
letters, and even fixed the hour of his suicide; then, at the
last moment, he had reconsidered. And always, at the
supreme moment, something unexpected may happen; con-
sequently no man can know when he will die.

"At one o'clock in the afternoon, Your Excellency!"
these amiable idiots had said to him. They had informed
him only because his death had been plotted; and yet he
was terrified simply to learn the hour when it might have
occurred. He admitted that they would kill him some
day or other, but it would not be the next day . . . it
would not be the next day, and he could sleep quietly, like
an immortal being. . . . The imbeciles! They did not
know what a gulf they had dug in saying, with stupid

amiability: "At one o'clock in the afternoon, Your Excellency!"

From the bitter anguish that shot through his heart, the Minister understood that he would know neither sleep, nor rest, nor joy, until this black and accursed hour, thus detached from the course of time, had passed. It was enough in itself to annihilate the light and enwrap the man in the opaque darkness of fear. Now that he was awake, the fear of death permeated his entire body, filtered into his bones, exuded from every pore.

Already the Minister had ceased to think of the assassins of the morrow: they had disappeared, forgotten in the multitude of inauspicious things that surrounded his life. He feared the unexpected, the inevitable: an attack of apoplexy, a laceration of the heart, the rupture of a little artery suddenly made powerless to resist the flow of blood and splitting like a glove on swollen hands.

His thick, short neck frightened him; he dared not look at his swollen fingers, full of some fatal fluid. And though, just before, in the darkness, he had been compelled to stir in order to avoid resemblance to a corpse, now, under this bright, cold, hostile, frightful light, it seemed to him horrible, impossible, to move even to light a cigarette or ring for a servant. His nerves were at a tension. With red and upturned eyes and burning head, he stifled.

Suddenly, in the darkness of the sleeping house, the electric bell just under the ceiling, among the dust and spiders' webs, became animate. Its little metallic tongue beat hurriedly against its sonorous edge. It stopped for a moment, and then began to ring again in a continuous and terrifying fashion.

People came running. Here and there lamps were lighted on the walls and chandeliers—too few of them for intense illumination, but enough to create shadows. On every hand appeared these shadows: they arose in the corners and stretched out upon the ceiling, fastening upon all projections and running along the walls. It was difficult to understand where all these taciturn, monstrous, and innumerable shadows could have kept themselves before—mute souls of mute things.

A thick and trembling voice said something indistinguishable. Then they telephoned to the doctor: the Minister was ill. His Excellency's wife was summoned also.

II

SENTENCED TO BE HANGED

THE predictions of the police were realized. Four terrorists, three men and one woman, carrying bombs, revolvers, and infernal machines, were taken in front of the
steps of the residence; a fifth accomplice was arrested at
her dwelling, where the implements had been manufactured
and the conspiracy planned. A large quantity of dynamite
and many weapons were found there. All five were very
young: the eldest of the men was twenty-eight, the younger
of the women nineteen. They were tried in the fortress
where they had been imprisoned after their arrest; they
were tried quickly and secretly, as was the custom at that
merciless epoch.

Before the court all five were calm, but serious and
thoughtful; their contempt for the judges was so great
that they did not care to emphasize their fearlessness by a
useless smile or a pretence of gaiety. They were just tranquil enough to protect their souls and the deep gloom of
their agony from the malevolent gaze of strangers. Some
questions they refused to answer, some they answered simply, briefly, precisely, as if they were speaking, not to
judges, but to statisticians desirous of completing tables of
figures. Three of them, one woman and two men, gave

their real names; two refused to disclose their identity, which remained unknown to the court. In everything that happened they manifested that distant and attenuated curiosity peculiar to people seriously ill or possessed by a single all-powerful idea. They cast swift glances, seized upon an interesting word in its flight, and went back to their thoughts, resuming them at the exact point where they had dropped them.

The accused placed nearest the judges had given his name as Sergey Golovin, a former officer, son of a retired colonel. He was very young, with broad shoulders, and so robust that neither the prison or the expectation of certain death had been able to dim the color of his cheeks or the expression of happy innocence in his blue eyes. Throughout the trial he twisted his thick blond beard, to which he had not yet become accustomed, and gazed steadily at the window, knitting his brows.

It was the latter part of winter, that period into which, among snowstorms and gray, cold days, the approaching spring projects sometimes, as a forerunner, a warm and luminous day, or even a single hour, so passionately young and sparkling that the sparrows in the street become mad with joy and men seem intoxicated. Now, through the upper window, still covered with the dust of the previous summer, a very odd and beautiful sky was to be seen; at the first glance it seemed a thick and milky gray; then, upon a second examination, it appeared to be covered with azure stains, of an ever-deepening blue, a blue pure and infinite. And because it did not strip itself suddenly, but modestly draped itself in the transparent veil of clouds, it became charming, like one's *fiancée*. Sergey Golovin looked at the sky, pulled at his mustache, winked now one and now the other of his eyes behind the long, heavy eyelashes, and reflected profoundly on nobody knows what. Once, even, his fingers moved rapidly, and an expression of naïve joy appeared upon his face; but he looked around him, and his joy was extinguished like a live coal upon which one steps. Almost instantaneously, almost without transition, the redness of his cheeks gave place to a corpse-like pallor; a fine hair painfully pulled out was pressed as in a vice between his bloodless finger-ends. But the joy of life and of the spring was still stronger. A few minutes later the young face resumed its naïve expression and sought again the sky of spring.

Toward the sky also looked an unknown young girl, surnamed Musya. She was younger than Golovin, but seemed his elder because of the severity, the gravity, of her proud and loyal eyes. The delicate neck and slender arms alone revealed that intangible something which is youth itself, and which sounded so distinctly in the pure harmonious voice that resembled a costly instrument in perfect tune. Musya was very pale, of that passionate pallor peculiar to those who burn with an inner, radiant, and powerful fire. She scarcely stirred; from time to time only, with a gesture that was hardly visible, she felt for a deep trace in the third finger of her right hand—the trace of a ring recently removed. She looked at the sky with calmness and indifference; she looked at it simply because everything

in this commonplace and dirty hall was hostile to her and
seemed to scrutinize her face. This bit of blue sky was the
only pure and true thing upon which she could look with
confidence.

The judges pitied Sergey Golovin and hated Musya.

Musya's neighbor, motionless also, with hands folded
between his knees and somewhat of affectation in his pose,
was an unknown surnamed Werner. If one can bolt a
face as one bolts a heavy door, the unknown had bolted
his as if it were a door of iron. He gazed steadily at the
floor, and it was impossible to tell whether he was calm
or deeply moved, whether he was thinking of something or
listening to the testimony of the policemen. He was rather
short of stature; his features were fine and noble. He gave
the impression of an immense and calm force, of a cold
and audacious valor. The very politeness with which he
uttered his clear and curt replies seemed dangerous on his
lips. On the backs of the other prisoners the customary
cloak seemed a ridiculous costume; on him it was not even
noticeable, so foreign was the garment to the man. Although Werner had been armed only with a poor revolver,
while the others carried bombs and infernal machines, the
judges looked upon him as the leader, and treated him
with a certain respect, with the same brevity which he employed toward them.

In his neighbor, Vasily Kashirin, a frightful moral struggle was going on between the intolerable terror of death
and the desperate desire to subdue this fear and conceal
it from the judges. Ever since the prisoners had been

taken to court in the morning, he had been stifling under the hurried beating of his heart. Drops of sweat appeared continually on his brow; his hands were moist and cold; his damp and icy shirt, sticking to his body, hindered his movements. By a superhuman effort of the will he kept his fingers from trembling, and maintained the firmness and moderation of his voice and the tranquillity of his gaze. He saw nothing around him; the sound of the voice that he heard seemed to reach him through a fog, and it was in a fog also that he stiffened himself in a desperate effort to answer firmly and aloud. But, as soon as he had spoken, he forgot the questions, as well as his own phrases; the silent and terrible struggle began again. And upon his person death was so in evidence that the judges turned their eyes away from him. It was as difficult to determine his age as that of a rotting corpse. According to his papers he was only twenty-three. Once or twice Werner touched him gently on the knee, and each time he answered briefly:

"It's nothing."

His hardest moment was when he suddenly felt an irresistible desire to utter inarticulate cries, like a hunted beast. Then he gave Werner a slight push; without raising his eyes, the latter answered in a low voice:

"It's nothing, Vasya. It will soon be over!"

Consumed by anxiety, Tanya Kovalchuk, the fifth terrorist, sheltered her comrades with a maternal look. She was still very young; her cheeks seemed as highly colored as those of Sergey Golovin; and yet she seemed to be the mother of all the accused, so full of tender anxiety and infinite love were her looks, her smile, her fear. The progress of the trial did not interest her. She listened to her comrades simply to see if their voices trembled, if they were afraid, if they needed water.

But she could not look at Vasya; his anguish was too intense; she contented herself with cracking her plump fingers. At Musya and Werner she gazed with proud and respectful admiration, her face then wearing a grave and serious expression. As for Sergey Golovin, she continually tried to attract his attention by her smile.

"The dear comrade, he is looking at the sky. Look, look!" thought she, as she observed the direction of his eyes.

"And Vasya? My God! My God! . . . What can be done to comfort him? If I speak to him, perhaps it will make matters worse; suppose he should begin to weep?"

Like a peaceful pool reflecting every wandering cloud, her amiable and clear countenance showed all the feelings and all the thoughts, however fleeting, of her four comrades. She forgot that she was on trial too and would be hanged; her indifference to this was absolute. It was in her dwelling that the bombs and dynamite had been found; strange as it may seem, she had received the police with pistol shots, and had wounded one of them in the head.

The trial ended toward eight o'clock, just as the day was drawing to its close. Little by little, in the eyes of Sergey and Musya, the blue sky disappeared; without reddening, without smiling, it grew dim gently as on a summer evening, becoming grayish, and suddenly cold and wintry. Golovin heaved a sigh, stretched himself, and raised his eyes toward the window, where the chilly darkness of the night was already making itself manifest; still pulling his beard, he began to examine the judges, the soldiers, and their weapons, exchanging a smile with Tanya Kovalchuk. As for Musya, when the sun had set completely, she did not lower her gaze to the ground, but directed it toward a corner where a spider's web was swaying gently in the invisible current of warm air from the stove; and thus she remained until the sentence had been pronounced.

After the verdict, the condemned said their farewells to their lawyers, avoiding their disconcerted, pitying, and confused looks; then they grouped themselves for a moment near the door, and exchanged short phrases.

"It's nothing, Vasya! All will soon be over!" said Werner.

"But there is nothing the matter with me, brother!" answered Kashirin, in a strong, quiet, and almost joyous voice. In fact, his face had taken on a slight color, no longer resembling that of a corpse.

"The devil take them! They have hanged us all just the same!" swore Golovin naïvely.

"It was to have been expected," answered Werner, without agitation.

"To-morrow the final judgment will be rendered, and they will put us all in the same cell," said Tanya, to console her comrades. "We shall remain together until the execution."

Silently, and with a resolute air, Musya started off.

III

"I MUST NOT BE HANGED"

A FORTNIGHT before the affair of the terrorists, in the same court, but before other judges, Ivan Yanson, a peasant, had been tried and sentenced to be hanged.

Ivan Yanson had been hired as a farm-hand by a well-to-do farmer, and was distinguished in no way from the other poor devils of his class. He was a native of Wesenberg, in Esthonia; for some years he had been advancing gradually toward the capital, passing from one farm to another. He had very little knowledge of Russian. As there were none of his countrymen living in the neighborhood, and as his employer was a Russian, named Lazaref, Yanson remained silent for almost two years. He said hardly a word to either man or beast. He led the horse to water and harnessed it without speaking to it, walking about it lazily, with short hesitating steps. When the horse began to run, Yanson did not say a word, but beat it cruelly with his enormous whip. Drink transformed his cold and wicked obstinacy into fury. The hissing of the lash and the regular and painful sound of his wooden shoes on the floor of the shed could be heard even at the farmhouse. To punish him for torturing the horse the farmer at first beat Yanson, but, not succeeding in correcting him, he gave it up.

Once or twice a month Yanson got drunk, especially when he took his master to the station. His employer once on board the train, Yanson drove a short distance away, and waited until the train had started.

Then he returned to the station, and got drunk at the buffet. He came back to the farm on the gallop, a distance of seven miles, beating the unfortunate beast unmercifully, giving it its head, and singing and shouting incomprehensible phrases in Esthonian. Sometimes silent, with set teeth, impelled by a whirlwind of indescribable fury, suffering, and enthusiasm, he was like a blind man in his mad career; he did not see the passers-by, he did not insult them, uphill and down he maintained his furious gait.

His master would have discharged him, but Yanson did not demand high wages, and his comrades were no better than he.

One day he received a letter written in Esthonian; but, as he did not know how to read or write, and as no one about him knew this language, Yanson threw it into the muck-heap with savage indifference, as if he did not understand that it brought him news from his native country. Probably needing a woman, he tried also to pay court to the girl employed on the farm. She repulsed him, for he was short and puny, and covered with hideous freckles; after that, he let her alone.

But, though he spoke little, Yanson listened continually. He listened to the desolate snow-covered fields, containing hillocks of frozen manure that resembled a series of little tombs heaped up by the snow; he listened to the bluish and limpid distance, the sonorous telegraph-poles. He alone knew what the fields and telegraph-poles were saying. He listened also to the conversation of men, the stories of murder, pillage, fire.

One night, in the village, the little church-bell began to ring in a feeble and lamentable way; flames appeared. Malefactors from nobody knew where were pillaging the neighboring farm. They killed the owner and his wife, and set fire to the house. This caused a feeling of anxiety on the farm where Yanson lived: day and night the dogs were loose; the master kept a gun within reach of his bed. He wished also to give an old weapon to Yanson, but the latter, after examining it, shook his head and refused it. The farmer did not understand that Yanson had more confidence in the efficacy of his Finnish knife than in this rusty old machine.

"It would kill me myself!" said he.

"You are only an imbecile, Ivan!"

And one winter evening, when the other farm-hand had gone to the station, this same Ivan Yanson, who was afraid of a gun, committed robbery and murder, and made an attempt at rape. He did it with an astonishing simplicity. After shutting the servant in the kitchen, lazily, like a man almost dead with sleep, he approached his master from behind, and stabbed him several times in the back. The master fell unconscious; his wife began to cry and to run about the chamber. Showing his teeth, and holding his knife in his hand, Yanson began to ransack trunks and drawers. He found the money; then, as if he had just seen the master's wife for the first time, he threw himself upon her to rape her, without the slightest premeditation. But he happened to drop his knife; and, as the woman was the stronger, she not only resisted Yanson, but half strangled him. At this moment the farmer recovered his senses, and the servant broke in the kitchen-door and came in. Yanson fled. They took him an hour later, squatting in the corner of the shed, and scratching matches which continually went out. He was trying to set fire to the farm.

A few days later the farmer died. Yanson was tried and sentenced to death. In the court one would have said that he did not understand what was going on; he viewed the large imposing hall without curiosity, and explored his nose with a shrunken finger that nothing disgusted. Only those who had seen him at church on Sunday could have guessed that he had done something in the way of making a toilet; he wore a knitted cravat of dirty red; in spots his hair was smooth and dark; in others it consisted of light thin locks, like wisps of straw on an uncultivated and devastated field.

When the sentence of death by hanging was pronounced, Yanson suddenly showed emotion. He turned scarlet, and began to untie and tie his cravat, as if it were choking him. Then he waved his arms without knowing why, and declared to the presiding judge, who had read the sentence:

"She has said that I must be hanged."

" 'She'? Who?" asked the presiding judge, in a deep bass voice.

Yanson pointed at the presiding judge with his finger, and, looking at him furtively, answered angrily:

"You!"

"Well?"

Again Yanson turned his eyes toward one of the judges, in whom he divined a friend, and repeated:

"She has said that I must be hanged. I must not be hanged."

"Take away the accused."

But Yanson still had time to repeat, in a grave tone of conviction:

"I must not be hanged."

And with his outstretched finger and irritated face, to which he tried in vain to give an air of gravity, he seemed so stupid that the guard, in violation of orders, said to him in an undertone as he led him away:

"Well, you are a famous imbecile, you are!"

"I must not be hanged!" repeated Yanson, obstinately.

They shut him up again in the cell in which he had passed a month, and to which he had become accustomed, as he had become accustomed to everything: to blows, to brandy, to the desolate and snow-covered country sown with rounded hillocks resembling tombs. It even gave him pleasure to see his bed again, and his grated window, and to eat what they gave him; he had taken nothing since morning. The disagreeable thing was what had happened in court, about which he knew not what to think. He had no idea at all of what death by hanging was like.

The guard said to him, in a tone of remonstrance:

"Well, brother, there you are, hanged!"

"And when will they hang me?" asked Yanson, in a tone of incredulity. The guard reflected.

"Ah! wait, brother; you must have companions; they do not disturb themselves for a single individual, and especially for a little fellow like you."

"Then, when?" insisted Yanson.

He was not offended that they did not want to take the trouble to hang him all alone; he did not believe in this excuse, and thought they simply wanted to put off the execution, and then pardon him.

"When? When?" resumed the guard. "It is not a question of hanging a dog, which one takes behind a shed and dispatches with a single blow! Is that what you would like, imbecile?"

"Why, no, I would not like it!" said Yanson suddenly, with a joyous grimace. "'Twas she that said I must be hanged, but I, I do not want to be hanged!"

And, for the first time in his life perhaps, he began to laugh—a grinning and stupid laugh, but terribly gay. He seemed like a goose beginning to quack. The guard looked at Yanson in astonishment, and then knitted his brows: this stupid gaiety on the part of a man who was to be executed insulted the prison, the gallows itself, and made them ridiculous. And suddenly it seemed to the old guard, who had passed all his life in prison and considered the laws of the gaol as those of nature, that the prison and all of life were a sort of mad-house in which he, the guard, was the chief madman.

"The devil take you!" said he, spitting on the ground. "Why do you show your teeth? This is no wine-shop!"

"And I, I do not want to be hanged! Ha! ha! ha!"

Yanson laughed always.

"Satan!" replied the guard, crossing himself.

All the evening Yanson was calm, and even joyous. He repeated the phrase that he had uttered: "I must not be hanged," and so convincing, so irrefutable was it that he had no occasion for anxiety. He had long since forgotten his crime; sometimes he simply regretted that he had not succeeded in raping the woman. Soon he thought no more about the matter.

Every morning Yanson asked when he would be hanged, and every morning the guard answered him angrily:

"You have time enough." And he went out quickly, before Yanson began to laugh.

Thanks to this invariable exchange of words, Yanson persuaded himself that the execution would never take place; for whole days he lay upon his bed, dreaming vaguely of the desolate and snow-covered fields, of the buffet at the railway station, and also of things farther away and more luminous. He was well fed in prison, he took on flesh.

"She would love me now," he said to himself, thinking of his master's wife. "Now I am as big as her husband."

He had only one desire—to drink brandy and course madly over the roads with his horse at full gallop.

When the terrorists were arrested, the whole prison learned of it. One day, when Yanson put his customary question, the guard answered him abruptly, in an irritated voice:

"It will be soon. In a week, I think."

Yanson turned pale; the gaze of his glassy eyes became so thick that he seemed as if asleep.

"You are joking?" he asked.

"Formerly you could not await the time, to-day you say that I am joking. No jokes are tolerated here. It is you who like jokes, but we do not tolerate them," replied the guard with dignity; then he went out.

When evening came, Yanson had grown thin. His skin, which had become smooth again for a few days, was contracted into a thousand little wrinkles. He took no notice of anything; his movements were made slowly, as if every toss of the head, every gesture of the arm, every step, were a difficult undertaking, that must first be deeply studied. During the night Yanson lay on his camp-bed, but his eyes did not close; they remained open until morning.

"Ah!" exclaimed the guard, on seeing him the next day.

With the satisfaction of the *savant* who has made a new and a successful experiment, he examined the condemned man attentively and without haste; now everything was proceeding in the usual fashion. Satan was covered with shame, the sanctity of the prison and of the gallows was re-established. Indulgent, and even full of sincere pity, the old man asked:

"Do you want to see someone?"

"Why?"

"To say good-bye, of course . . . to your mother, for instance, or to your brother."

"I must not be hanged," said Yanson in a low voice, casting a glance sidewise at the gaoler. "I do not want to be hanged."

The guard looked at him, without saying a word.

Yanson was a little calmer in the evening. The day was so ordinary, the cloudy winter sky shone in so usual a fashion, so familiar was the sound of steps and conversations in the corridor, that he ceased to believe in the execution. Formerly the night had been to him simply the moment of darkness, the time for sleep. But now he was conscious of its mysterious and menacing essence. To disbelieve in death one must see and hear about one the customary course of life: steps, voices, light. And now everything seemed extraordinary to him; this silence, these shades, that seemed to be already the shades of death; already he felt the approach of inevitable death; in bewilderment he climbed the first steps of the gibbet.

The day, the night, brought him alternations of hope and fear; and so things went until the evening when he felt, or understood, that the inevitable death would come three days later, at sunrise.

He had never thought of death; for him it had no shape. But now he felt plainly that it had entered his cell, and was groping about in search of him. To escape it he began to run.

The room was so small that the corners seemed to push him back toward the centre. He could not hide himself anywhere. Several times he struck the walls with his body; once he hurled himself against the door. He staggered and fell, with his face upon the ground; he felt the grasp of death upon him. Glued to the floor, his face touching the dirty black asphalt, Yanson screamed with terror until help came. When they had lifted him up, seated him on his bed, and sprinkled him with cold water, he did not dare to open both eyes. He half opened one, perceived an empty and luminous corner of his cell, and began again to scream.

But the cold water had its effect. The guard, moreover, always the same old man, slapped Yanson several times on the head in a fatherly fashion. This sensation of life drove out the thought of death. Yanson slept deeply the rest of the night. He lay on his back, with mouth open, snoring loud and long. Between his half-closed eyelids appeared a whitish, flat, and dead eye, without a pupil.

Then day, night, voices, steps, the cabbage soup, everything became for him one continuous horror that plunged him into a state of wild astonishment. His weak mind could not reconcile the monstrous contradiction between, on the one hand, the bright light and the odor of the cabbage, and, on the other, the fact that two days later he must die. He thought of nothing; he did not even count the hours; he was simply the prey of a dumb terror in presence of this contradiction that bewildered his brain: to-day life, to-morrow death. He ate nothing, he slept no more; he sat timidly all night long on a stool, with his legs crossed under him, or else he walked up and down his cell with furtive steps. He appeared to be in a state of open-mouthed astonishment; before taking the most common-place article into his hands he would examine it suspiciously.

The gaolers ceased to pay attention to him. His was the ordinary condition of the condemned man, resembling, according to his gaoler who had not experienced it himself, that of an ox felled by a club.

"He is stunned; now he will feel nothing more until the moment of death," said the guard, examining him with his experienced eye. "Ivan, do you hear? Ho there, Ivan!"

"I must not be hanged!" answered Yanson, in a colorless voice; his lower jaw had dropped.

"If you had not killed, they would not hang you," reproachfully said the chief gaoler, a highly important young man, wearing a decoration. "To steal, you have killed, and you do not want to be hanged!"

"I do not want to be hanged!" replied Yanson.

"Well, you don't have to want to; that's your affair. But, instead of talking nonsense, you would do better to dispose of your possessions. You surely must have something."

"He has nothing at all! A shirt and a pair of pantaloons! And a fur cap!"

Thus time passed until Thursday. And Thursday, at midnight, a large number of people entered Yanson's cell; a man with cloth epaulets said to him:

"Get ready! it is time to start."

Always with the same slowness and the same indolence

Yanson dressed himself in all that he possessed, and tied his dirty shawl around his neck. While watching him dress, the man with the epaulets, who was smoking a cigarette, said to one of the assistants:

"How warm it is to-day! It is spring!"

Yanson's eyes closed; he was in a complete drowse. The guard shouted:

"Come, come! Make haste! You are going to sleep!"

Suddenly Yanson ceased to move.

"I must not be hanged," said he, with indolence.

He began to walk submissively, shrugging his shoulders. In the courtyard the moist spring air had a sudden effect upon him; his nose began to run; it was thawing; close by, drops of water were falling with a joyous sound. While the gendarmes were getting into the unlighted vehicle, bending over and rattling their swords, Yanson lazily passed his finger under his running nose, or arranged his badly-tied shawl.

IV

WE OF OREL

THE court that had tried Yanson sentenced to death at the same session Michael Goloubetz, known as Michka the Tzigane, a peasant of the department of Orel, district of Eletz. The last crime of which they accused him, with evidence in support of the charge, was robbery, followed by the assassination of three persons. As for his past, it was unknown. There were vague indications to warrant the belief that the Tzigane had taken part in a whole series of other murders. With absolute sincerity and frankness he termed himself a brigand, and overwhelmed with his irony those who, to follow the fashion, pompously styled themselves "expropriators"; his last crime he described willingly in all its details. But, at the slightest reference to the past, he answered:

"Go ask the wind that blows over the fields!"

And, if they persisted in questioning him, the Tzigane assumed a dignified and serious air.

"We of Orel are all hot-heads, the fathers of all the robbers of the world," said he, in a sedate and judicial tone.

They had nicknamed him Tzigane because of his physiognomy and his thieving habits. He was thin and strangely dark; yellow spots outlined themselves upon his cheek-bones which were as prominent as those of a Tartar. He had a way of rolling the whites of his eyes, that reminded one of a horse. His gaze was quick and keen, full of curiosity, terrifying. The things over which his swift glance passed seemed to lose something or other, and to become transformed by surrendering to him part of themselves. One hesitated to take a cigarette that he had looked at, as if it had already been in his mouth. His extraordinarily mobile nature made him seem now to coil and concentrate himself like a twisted handkerchief, now to scatter himself like a sheaf of sparks. He drank water almost by the pailful, like a horse.

When the judges questioned him, he raised his head quickly, and answered without hesitation, even with satisfaction:

"It is true!"

Sometimes, to lend emphasis, he rolled his "r's" vigorously.

Suddenly he jumped to his feet, and said to the presiding judge:

"Permit me to whistle?"

"Why?" exclaimed the judge, in astonishment.

"The witnesses say that I gave the signal to my comrades; I will show you how I did it. It is very interesting."

A little disconcerted, the judge granted the desired permission. The Tzigane quickly placed four fingers in his mouth, two of each hand; he rolled his eyes furiously. And the inanimate air of the court-room was rent by a truly savage whistle. There was everything in the piercing sound, partly human, partly animal; the mortal anguish of the victim, and the savage joy of the assassin; a threat, a call, and the tragic solitude, the darkness, of a rainy autumn night.

The judge shook his hand; with docility the Tzigane stopped. Like an artist who has just played a difficult air with assured success, he sat down, wiped his wet fingers on his cloak, and looked at the spectators with a satisfied air.

"What a brigand!" exclaimed one of the judges, rubbing his ear. But another, who had Tartar eyes, like the Tzigane's, was looking dreamily into the distance, over the brigand's head; he smiled, and replied:

"It was really interesting."

Without remorse, the judges sentenced the Tzigane to death.

"It is just!" said the Tzigane, when the sentence had been pronounced.

And, turning to a soldier of the guard, he added with an air of bravado:

"Well, let us be off, imbecile! And keep a good hold of your gun, lest I snatch it from you!"

The soldier looked at him seriously and timidly; he exchanged a glance with his comrade, and tested his weapon to see if it was in working order. The other did the same. And all the way to the prison it seemed to the soldiers that they did not walk, but flew; they were so absorbed by the condemned man that they were unconscious of the route, of the weather, and of themselves.

Like Yanson, Michka the Tzigane remained seventeen days in prison before being executed. And the seventeen days passed as rapidly as a single day, filled with a single thought, that of flight, of liberty, of life. The turbulent and incoercible spirit of the Tzigane, stifled by the walls, the gratings, and the opaque window through which nothing could be seen, employed all its force in setting Michka's brain on fire. As in a vapor of intoxication, bright but incomplete images whirled, clashed, and mingled in his head; they passed with a blinding and irresistible rapidity, and they all tended to the same end: flight, liberty, life. For entire hours, with nostrils distended like those of a horse, the Tzigane sniffed the air; it seemed to him that he inhaled the odor of hemp and flame, of dense smoke. Or else he turned in his cell like a top, examining the walls, feeling them with his fingers, measuring them, piercing the ceiling with his gaze, sawing the bars in his mind. His agitation was a source of torture to the soldier who watched him through the window; several times he threatened to fire on him.

During the night the Tzigane slept deeply, almost without stirring, in an invariable but living immobility, like a temporarily inactive spring. But, as soon as he jumped to his feet, he began again to plan, to grope, to study. His hands were always dry and hot. Sometimes his heart suddenly congealed, as if they had placed in his breast a new block of ice which did not melt, and which caused a continuous shiver to run over his skin. At these times his naturally dark complexion became darker still, taking on the blue-black shade of bronze. Then a queer tic seized him; he constantly licked his lips, as if he had eaten a dish that was much too sweet; then, with a hiss, and with set teeth, he spat upon the ground the saliva that had thus accumulated in his mouth. He left his words unfinished; his thoughts ran so fast that his tongue could no longer keep up with them.

One day the chief of the guards entered his cell, accompanied by a soldier. He squinted at the spittle with which the ground was spattered, and said rudely:

"See how he has dirtied his cell!"

The Tzigane replied quickly:

"And you, you ugly mug, you have soiled the whole earth, and I haven't said a word to you. Why do you annoy me?"

With the same rudeness the chief of the guards offered him the post of hangman. The Tzigane showed his teeth, and began to laugh:

"So they can find none! That's not bad! Go on then hanging people! Ah! Ah! There are necks and ropes, and nobody to do the hanging! My God, that's not bad."

"They will give your life as a reward!"

"I should say so: I could hardly play the hangman after I am dead!"

"Well, what do you say, yes or no?"

"And how do they hang here? They probably choke people secretly."

"No, they hang them to music!" retorted the chief.

"Imbecile! Of course there must be music . . . like this. . . ."

And he began to sing a captivating air.

"You have gone completely mad, my friend!" said the guard. "Come, speak seriously, what is your decision?"

The Tzigane showed his teeth.

"Are you in a hurry? Come back later, and I will tell you!"

And to the chaos of unfinished images which overwhelmed the Tzigane was added a new idea: how agreeable it would be to be the headsman! He clearly pictured to himself the square black with people, and the scaffold on which he, the Tzigane, walked back and forth, in a red shirt, with axe in hand. The sun illuminates the heads, plays gaily on the axe blade; everything is so joyous, so sumptuous, that even he whose head is to be cut off smiles. Behind the crowd are to be seen the carts and the noses of the horses; the peasants have come to town for the occasion. Still farther away fields. The Tzigane licked his lips, and spat upon the ground. Suddenly it seemed to him that his fur cap had just been pulled down over his mouth; everything became dark; he gasped for breath; and his heart changed into a block of ice, while little shivers ran through his body.

Twice more the chief came back; the Tzigane, showing his teeth again, answered:

"What a hurry you are in! Come back another time!"

Finally, one day, the gaoler cried to him, as he was passing by the window:

"You have lost your chance, my ill-favoured raven. They have found another."

"The devil take you! Go, be the hangman yourself!"
replied the Tzigane. And he ceased to dream of the splendors of his trade.

But toward the end, the nearer drew the day of execution, the more intolerable became the impetuosity of the torn images. The Tzigane would have liked to wait, to halt, but the furious torrent carried him on, giving him no chance to get a hold on anything; for everything was in a whirl. And his sleep became agitated; he had new and shapeless visions, as badly squared as painted blocks, and even more impetuous than his thoughts had been. It was no longer a torrent, but a continual fall from an infinite height, a whirling flight through the whole world of colors. Formerly the Tzigane had worn only a mustache tolerably well cared for; in prison he had been obliged to grow his beard, which was short, black, and stubbly, giving him a crazy look. There were moments, in fact, when the Tzigane lost his mind. He turned about in his cell all unconscious of his movements, continuing to feel for the rough and uneven walls. And he always drank great quantities of water, like a horse.

One evening, when they were lighting the lamps, the Tzigane dropped on all fours in the middle of his cell, and began to howl like a wolf. He did this very seriously, as if performing an indispensable and important act. He filled his lungs with air, and then expelled it slowly in a prolonged and trembling howl. With knit brows, he listened to himself attentively. The very trembling of the voice seemed a little affected; he did not shout indistinctly;

he made each note in this wild beast's cry sound separately, full of unspeakable suffering and terror.

Suddenly he stopped, and remained silent for a few minutes, without getting up. He began to whisper, as if speaking to the ground:

"Dear friends, good friends . . . dear friends . . . good friends . . . have pit . . . friends! My friends!"

He said a word, and listened to it.

He jumped to his feet, and for a whole hour poured forth a steady stream of the worst curses.

"Go to the devil, you scoundrels!" he screamed, rolling his bloodshot eyes. "If I must be hanged, hang me, instead of . . . Ah, you blackguards!"

The soldier on guard, as white as chalk, wept with anguish and fear; he pounded the door with the muzzle of his gun, and cried in a lamentable voice:

"I will shoot you! By God, do you hear? I will shoot you!"

But he did not dare to fire; they never fire on prisoners sentenced to death, except in case of revolt. And the Tzigane ground his teeth, swore, and spat. His brain, placed on the narrow frontier that separates life from death, crumbled like a lump of dried clay.

When they came, during the night, to take him to the gallows, he regained a little of his animation. His cheeks took on some color; in his eyes the usual strategy, a little savage, sparkled again, and he asked of one of the functionaries:

"Who will hang us? The new one? Is he accustomed to it yet?"

"You needn't disturb yourself about that," answered the personage thus appealed to.

"What? Not disturb myself! It is not Your Highness that is going to be hanged, but I! At least don't spare the soap on the slip-noose; the State pays for it!"

"I beg you to hold your tongue!"

"This fellow, you see, consumes all the soap in the prison; see how his face shines," continued the Tzigane, pointing to the chief of the guards.

"Silence!"

"Don't spare the soap!"

Suddenly he began to laugh, and his legs became numb. Yet, when he arrived in the court-yard, he could still cry:

"Say, there! you fellows yonder, come forward with my carriage!"

V

"KISS HIM AND BE SILENT"

THE verdict against the five terrorists was pronounced in its final form and confirmed the same day. The condemned were not notified of the day of execution. But they foresaw that they would be hanged, according to custom, the same night, or, at the latest, the night following. When they were offered the opportunity of seeing their families the next day, they understood that the execution was fixed for Friday at daybreak.

Tanya Kovalchuk had no near relatives. She knew only of some distant relatives living in Little Russia, who probably knew nothing of the trial or the verdict. Musya and Werner, not having revealed their identity, did not insist on seeing any of their people. Only Sergey Golovin and Vasily Kashirin were to see their families. The thought of this approaching interview was frightful to both of them, but they could not make up their minds to refuse a final conversation, a last kiss.

Sergey Golovin thought sadly of this visit. He was fond of his father and mother; he had seen them very recently, and he was filled with terror at the thought of what was going to happen. The hanging itself, in all its monstrosity,

.in its disconcerting madness, outlined itself more readily in his imagination than these few short, incomprehensible minutes, that seemed apart from time, apart from life. What to do? What to say? The most simple and customary gestures—to shake hands, embrace, and say "How do you do, father?"—seemed to him frightful in their monstrous, inhuman, insane insignificance.

After the verdict they did not put the condemned in the same cell, as Tanya expected them to do. All the morning, up to the time when he received his parents, Sergey Golovin walked back and forth in his cell, twisting his short beard, his features pitiably contracted. Sometimes he stopped suddenly, filled his lungs with air, and puffed like a swimmer who has remained too long under water. But, as he was in good health, and as his young life was solidly implanted within him, even in these minutes of atrocious suffering, the blood coursed under his skin, coloring his cheeks; his blue eyes preserved their usual brilliancy.

Everything went off better than Sergey expected; his father, Nicolas Sergiévitch Golovin, a retired colonel, was the first to enter the room where the visitors were received. Evrything about him was white and of the same whiteness: face, hair, beard, hands. His old and well-brushed garment smelt of benzine; his epaulets seemed new. He entered with a firm and measured step, straightening himself up. Extending his dry, white hand, he said aloud:

"How do you do, Sergey?"

Behind him came the mother, with short steps; she

wore a strange smile. But she too shook hands with her son, and repeated aloud:

"How do you do, my little Sergey?"

She kissed him and sat down without saying a word. She did not throw herself upon her son, she did not begin to weep or cry, as Sergey expected her to do. She kissed him and sat down without speaking. With a trembling hand she even smoothed the wrinkles in her black silk gown.

Sergey did not know that the colonel had spent the entire previous night in rehearsing this interview. "We must lighten the last moments of our son's life, and not make them more painful for him," the colonel had decided; and he had carefully weighed each phrase, each gesture, of the morrow's visit. But sometimes, in the course of the rehearsal, he became confused, he forgot what he had prepared himself to say, and he wept bitterly, sunk in the corner of his sofa. The next morning he had explained to his wife what she was to do.

"Above all, kiss him and be silent," he repeated. "You will be able to speak later, a little later; but, after kissing him, be silent. Do not speak immediately after kissing him, do you understand? Otherwise you will say what you should not."

"I understand, Nicolas Sergiévitch!" answered the mother, with tears.

"And do not weep! May God keep you from that! Do not weep! You will kill him if you weep, mother!"

"And why do you weep yourself?"

"Why should one not weep here with the rest of you? You must not weep, do you hear?"

"All right, Nicolas Sergiévitch."

They got into a cab and started off, silent, bent, old; they were plunged in their thoughts amid the gay roar of the city; it was the carnival season, and the streets were filled with a noisy crowd.

They sat down. The colonel assumed a suitable attitude, his right hand thrust in the front of his frock-coat. Sergey remained seated a moment; his look met his mother's wrinkled face; he rose suddenly.

"Sit down, my little Sergey!" begged the mother.

"Sit down, Sergey!" repeated the father.

They kept silence. The mother wore a strange smile.

"How many moves we have made in your behalf, Sergey! Your father . . ."

"It was useless, my little mother!"

The colonel said, firmly:

"We were in duty bound to do it that you might not think that your parents had abandoned you."

Again they became silent. They were afraid to utter a syllable, as if each word of the language had lost its proper meaning and now meant but one thing: death. Sergey looked at the neat little frock-coat smelling of benzine, and thought: "He has no orderly now; then he must have cleaned his coat himself. How is it that I have never seen him clean his coat? Probably he does it in the morning." Suddenly he asked:

"And my sister? Is she well?"

"Ninotchka knows nothing!" answered the mother, quickly.

But the colonel sternly interrupted her:

"What is the use of lying? She has read the newspaper . . . let Sergey know that . . . all . . . his own . . . have thought . . . and . . ."

Unable to continue, he stopped. Suddenly the mother's face contracted, her features became confused and wild. Her colorless eyes were madly distended; more and more she panted for breath.

"Se . . . Ser . . . Ser . . . Ser . . ." she repeated, without moving her lips; "Ser . . ."

"My little mother!"

The colonel took a step; trembling all over, without knowing how frightful he was in his corpse-like pallor, in his desperate and forced firmness, he said to his wife:

"Be silent! Do not torture him! Do not torture him! Do not torture him! He must die! Do not torture him!"

Frightened, she was silent already, and he continued to repeat, with his trembling hands pressed against his breast:

"Do not torture him!"

Then he took a step backward, and again thrust his hand into the front of his frock-coat; wearing an expression of forced calmness, he asked aloud, with pallid lips:

"When?"

"To-morrow morning," answered Sergey.

The mother looked at the ground, biting her lips, as if she heard nothing. And she seemed to continue to bite her lips as she let fall these simple words:

"Ninotchka told me to kiss you, my little Sergey!"

"Kiss her for me!" said the condemned man.

"Good! The Chvostofs send their salutations. . . ."

"Who are they? Ah! yes. . . ."

The colonel interrupted him:

"Well, we must start. Rise, mother, it is necessary!"

The two men lifted the swooning woman.

"Bid him farewell!" ordered the colonel. "Give him your blessing!"

She did everything that she was told. But, while giving her son a short kiss and making on his person the sign of the cross, she shook her head and repeated distractedly:

"No, it is not that! No, it is not that!"

"Adieu, Sergey!" said the father. They shook hands, and exchanged a short, but earnest, kiss.

"You . . . " began Sergey.

"Well?" asked the father, spasmodically.

"No, not like that. No, no! What shall I say?" repeated the mother, shaking her head.

She had sat down again, and was tottering.

"You . . ." resumed Sergey. Suddenly his face took on a lamentable expression, and he grimaced like a child, tears filling his eyes. Through their sparkling facets he saw beside him the pale face of his father, who was weeping also.

"Father, you are a strong man!"

"What do you say? What do you say?" said the bewildered colonel. Suddenly, as if completely broken, he fell, with his head on his son's shoulder. And the two covered each other with ardent kisses, the father receiving them on his light hair, the prisoner on his cloak.

"And I?" asked suddenly a hoarse voice.

They looked: the mother was on her feet again, and, with her head thrown back, was watching them wrathfully, almost hatefully.

"What is the matter with you, mother?" cried the colonel.

"And I?" she repeated, shaking her head with an insane energy. "You embrace each other, and I? You are men, are you not? And I? and I? . . ."

"Mother!" and Sergey threw himself into her arms.

The last words of the colonel were:

"My blessing for your death, Sergey! Die with courage, like an officer!"

And they went away. . . . On returning to his cell Sergey lay upon his camp-bed, with face turned toward the wall that the soldiers might not see him, and wept a long time.

· · · · · * · · ·

Vasily Kashirin's mother came alone to visit him. The father, a rich merchant, had refused to accompany her. When the old woman entered, Vasily was walking in his cell. In spite of the heat, he was trembling with cold. The conversation was short and painful.

"You ought not to have come, mother. Why should we two torment each other?"

"Why all this, Vasya? Why have you done this, my son? God! God!"

The old woman began to weep, drying her tears with her black silk neckerchief.

Accustomed as they were, his brothers and he, to treat their mother roughly, she being a simple woman who did not understand them, he stopped, and, in the midst of his shivering, said to her, harshly:

"That's it, I knew how it would be. You understand nothing, mama, nothing!"

"Very well, my son. What is the matter with you? Are you cold?"

"I am cold," answered Vasily, and he began to walk again, looking sidewise now and then at the old woman with the same air of irritation.

"You are cold, my son . . ."

"Ah! You speak of cold, but soon . . ." He made a gesture of desperation.

Again the mother began to sob.

"I said to your father: 'Go to see him, he is your son, your flesh; give him a last farewell.' He would not."

"The devil take him! He is not a father. All his life he has been a scoundrel. He remains one!"

"Yet, Vasya, he is your father. . . ."

And the old woman shook her head reproachfully.

It was ridiculous and terrible. This paltry and useless conversation engaged them when face to face with death. While almost weeping, so sad was the situation, Vasily cried out:

"Understand then, mother. They are going to hang me, to hang me! Do you understand, yes or no?"

"And why did you kill?" she cried.

"My God! What are you saying? Even the beasts have feelings. Am I your son or not?"

He sat down and wept. His mother wept also; but, in their incapability of communicating in the same affection in order to face the terror of the approaching death, they wept cold tears that did not warm the heart.

"You ask me if I am your mother? You heap reproaches on me; and yet I have turned completely white these last few days."

"All right, all right, forgive me. Adieu! Embrace my brothers for me."

"Am I not your mother? Do I not suffer for you?"

At last she departed. She was weeping so that she could not see her way. And, the farther she got from the prison, the more abundant became her tears. She retraced her steps, losing herself in this city in which she was born, in which she had grown up, in which she had grown old. She entered a little abandoned garden, and sat down on a damp bench.

And suddenly she understood: to-morrow they would hang her son! She sprang to her feet, and tried to shout and run, but suddenly her head turned, and she sank to the earth. The path, white with frost, was wet and slippery; the old woman could not rise again. She rested her weight on her wrists, and then fell back again. The black neckerchief slipped from her head, uncovering her dirty gray hair. It seemed to her that she was celebrating her son's wedding. Yes, they had just married him, and she had drunk a little wine; she was slightly intoxicated.

"I cannot help myself! My God, I cannot help myself!"

And, with swinging head, she said to herself that she had drunk too much, and was crawling around on the wet ground, . . . but they gave her wine to drink, and wine again, and still more wine. And from her heart arose the laugh of the drunkard and the desire to abandon herself to a wild dance; . . . but they kept on lifting cups to her lips, one after another, one after another.

VI

THE HOURS FLY

In the fortress where the condemned terrorists were confined there was a steeple with an old clock. Every hour, every half-hour, every quarter of an hour, this clock struck in a tone of infinite sadness, like the distant and plaintive cry of birds of passage. In the daytime this odd and desolate music was lost in the noise of the city, of the broad and animated street that passed the fortress. The tramways rumbled, the shoes of the horses rattled, the trembling automobiles sounded their hoarse horns far into the distance. As the carnival was approaching, the peasants of the suburbs had come to town to earn some money as cab-drivers; the bells of the little Russian horses tinkled noisily. The conversations were gay, and had a flavor of intoxication, real holiday conversations. The weather harmonized with the occasion; the spring had brought a thaw, and the road was wet with dirty puddles. The trees on the squares had suddenly darkened. A slightly warm wind was blowing from the sea in copious moist puffs—a light, fresh air that seemed to have started on a joyous flight toward the infinite.

By night the street was silent under the brilliancy of the large electric suns. The immense fortress with its smooth walls was plunged in darkness and silence; a barrier of calm and shadow separated it from the ever-living city. Then they heard the striking of the hours, the slow, sad birth and death of a strange melody, foreign to the land.

Like big drops of transparent glass, the hours and the minutes fell from an immeasurable height into a metallic basin that was vibrating gently. Sometimes they were like birds that passed.

Into the cells came, day and night, this single sound. It penetrated through the roof, through the thick stone walls; it alone broke the silence. Sometimes they forgot it, or did not hear it. Sometimes they awaited it with despair; they lived only by and for this sound, having learned to be distrustful of silence. The prison was reserved for criminals of note; its special, rigorous regulations were as rigid and sharp as the corners of the walls. If there is nobility in cruelty, then the solemn, deaf, dead silence that caught up every breath and every rustle was noble.

In this silence, penetrated by the desolate striking of the flying minutes, three men and two women, separated from the world, were awaiting the coming of the night, of the dawn, and of the execution; and each was preparing for it in his own fashion.

Throughout her life Tanya Kovalchuk had thought only of others, and now also it was for her comrades that she underwent suffering and torture. She pictured death to herself only because it threatened Sergey Golovin, Musya, and the others; but her thoughts did not dwell on the fact that she too would be executed.

As if to reward herself for the artificial firmness that she had shown before the judges, she wept for hours altogether. This is characteristic of old women who have suffered much. When it occurred to her that Sergey might be un-

provided with tobacco, or that Werner possibly was deprived of the tea of which he was so fond—and this at
the moment that they were about to die—she suffered perhaps as much as at the idea of the execution. The execution
was something inevitable, even incidental, not worthy of
consideration; but that an imprisoned man should be without tobacco on the very eve of his execution was an idea
absolutely intolerable. Evoking the pleasant memories of
their common life, she lamented over the interview between
Sergey and his parents.

For Musya she felt a special pity. For a long time it
had seemed to her, mistakenly, however, that Musya was in
love with Werner; she had beautiful and luminous dreams
for their future. Before her arrest Musya wore a silver ring
on which were engraved a skull and crossbones surrounded
with a crown of thorns. Often Tanya Kovalchuk had
looked at this ring sorrowfully, viewing it as a symbol of
renunciation; half serious, half joking, she had asked Musya
to take it off.

"No, Tanya, I will not give it to you. You will soon have
another on your finger!"

Her comrades always thought that she would soon be
married, which much offended her. She wanted no husband. And, as she recalled these conversations with Musya
and reflected that Musya was indeed sacrificed, Tanya, full
of motherly pity, felt the tears choking her. Every time
the clock struck, she lifted her face, covered with tears,
and listened, wondering how this plaintive and persistent
summons of death was being received in the other cells.

VII

THERE IS NO DEATH

AND Musya was happy!

With arms folded behind her back, dressed in a prisoner's gown that was too large for her and that made her look like a youth wearing a borrowed costume, she walked back and forth in her cell, at a regular pace, never wearying. She had tucked up the long sleeves of her gown, and her thin and emaciated arms, the arms of a child, emerged from the flaring breadths like flower-stems from a coarse and unclean pitcher. The roughness of the stuff irritated the skin of her white and slender neck; sometimes, with her two hands, she released her throat, and felt cautiously for the spot where her skin was burning.

Musya walked with a long stride, and tried blushingly to justify to herself the fact that the finest of deaths, reserved hitherto for martyrs, had been assigned to her, so young, so humble, and who had done so little. It seemed to her that, in dying upon the scaffold, she was making a pretentious show that was in bad taste.

At her last interview with her lawyer she had asked him to procure poison for her, but immediately had given up the idea: would not people think that she was actuated by fear or by ostentation? Instead of dying modestly and unnoticed, would she not cause still further scandal? And she had added, quickly:

"No, no, it is useless!"

Now her sole desire was to explain, to prove, that she was not a heroine, that it was not a frightful thing to die, and that no one need pity her or worry on her account.

Musya sought excuses, pretexts of such a nature as to exalt her sacrifice and give it a real value, as if it had actually been called in question.

"In fact," she said to herself, "I am young; I might have lived for a long time. But . . ."

Just as the gleam of a candle is effaced by the radiance of the rising sun, youth and life seem to her dull and sombre beside the magnificent and luminous halo that is about to crown her modest person.

"Is it possible?" Musya asks herself, in great confusion. "Is it possible that I am worth anybody's tears?"

And she is seized with an unspeakable joy. There is no more doubt; she has been taken into the pale. She has a right to figure among the heroes who from all countries go to heaven through flames and executions. What serene peace, what infinite happiness! An immaterial being, she believes herself hovering in a divine light.

Of what else was Musya thinking? Of many things, since for her the thread of life was not severed by death but continued to unroll in a calm and regular fashion. She was thinking of her comrades, of those who at a distance were filled with anguish at the idea of her approaching execution, of those who nearer at hand would go with her

to the gallows. She was astonished that Vasily should be
a prey to terror, he who had always been brave. On Tuesday morning, when they had prepared themselves to kill,
and then to die themselves, Tanya Kovalchuk had trembled
with emotion; they had been obliged to send her away,
whereas Vasily joked and laughed and moved about amid
the bombs with so little caution that Werner had said to
him severely:

"One should not play with death!"

Why, then, was Vasily afraid now? And this incomprehensible terror was so foreign to Musya's soul that she
soon ceased to think about it and to inquire into its cause.
Suddenly she felt a mad desire to see Sergey Golovin and
laugh with him.

Perhaps too her thought was unwilling to dwell long on
the same subject, resembling therein a light bird that hovers
before infinite horizons, all space, the caressing and tender
azure, being accessible to it. The hours continued to strike.
Thoughts blended in this harmonious and distant symphony; fleeting images became a sort of music. It seemed
to Musya that she was travelling on a broad and easy
road in a quiet night; the carriage rode easily on its springs.
All care had vanished; the tired body was dissolved in the
darkness; joyous and weary, the thought peacefully created
vivid images, and became intoxicated on their beauty.
Musya recalled three comrades who had been hanged lately;
their faces were illuminated and near, nearer than those of
the living. . . . So in the morning one thinks gaily of the
hospitable friends who will receive you in the evening with
smiles on their lips.

At last Musya became weary from walking. She lay down cautiously on the camp-bed and continued to dream, with half-closed eyes.

"Is this really death? My God, how beautiful it is! Or is it life? I do not know, I do not know! I am going to see and hear. . . ."

From the first days of her imprisonment she had been a prey to hallucinations. She had a very musical ear; her sense of hearing, sharpened by the silence, gathered in the slightest echoes of life; the footsteps of the sentinels in the corridor, the striking of the clock, the whispering of the wind over the zinc roof, the creaking of a lantern, all blended for her in a vast and mysterious symphony. At first the hallucinations frightened Musya, and she drove them away as morbid manifestations; then, perceiving that she was in good health and had no pathological symptoms, she ceased to resist.

But now she hears very plainly the sound of the military band. She opens her eyes in astonishment, and raises her head. Through the windows she sees the night; the clock strikes. "Again!" she thought, as she closed her eyes without disturbing herself. Again the music begins. Musya clearly distinguishes the steps of the soldiers as they turn the corner of the prison; a whole regiment is passing before her windows. The boots keep time to the music on the frozen ground; one! two! one! two! Sometimes a boot squeaks; a foot slips and then recovers itself. The music draws nearer; it is playing a noisy and stirring triumphal march which Musya does not know. There is probably some festival in the fortress.

The soldiers are under her windows, and the cell is filled with joyous, regular, and harmonious sounds. A big brass trumpet emits false notes: it is not in time; now it is in advance, now it lags behind in a ridiculous fashion. Musya pictures to herself a little soldier playing this trumpet assiduously, and she laughs.

The regiment has passed; the sound of the footsteps grows fainter and fainter; one! two! one! two! In the distance the music becomes gayer and more beautiful. Several times more the trumpet sounds out of time, with its metallic, sonorous, and gay voice, and then all is quiet. Again the clock in the steeple strikes the hours.

New forms come and lean over her, surrounding her with transparent clouds and lifting her to a great height, where birds of prey are hovering. At left and right, above and below, everywhere birds are crying like heralds; they call, they warn. They spread their wings, and immensity sustains them. And on their inflated breasts that split the air is reflected the sparkling azure. The beating of Musya's heart becomes more and more regular, her respiration more and more calm and peaceful. She sleeps; her face is pale; her features are drawn; there are dark rings around her eyes. On her lips a smile. To-morrow, when the sun shall rise, this intelligent and fine face will be deformed by a grimace in which no trace of the human will be left; the brain will be inundated with thick blood; the glassy eyes will protrude from their orbits. But to-day Musya sleeps quietly, and smiles in her immortality.

Musya sleeps.

And the prison continues to live its special, blind, vigilant life, a sort of perpetual anxiety. They walk. They whisper. A gun rings out. It seems as if someone cries out. Is this reality or hallucination?

The grating in the door lowers noiselessly. In the dark opening appears a sinister bearded face. For a long time the widely-opened eyes view with astonishment the sleeping Musya; then the face disappears as quietly as it came.

The bells in the steeple ring and sing interminably. One would say that the weary hours were climbing a high mountain toward midnight. The ascent grows more and more painful. They slip, fall back with a groan, and begin again to toil painfully toward the black summit.

There is a sound of foosteps. Whispering voices are heard. Already they are harnessing the horses to the sombre, unlighted vehicle.

VIII

DEATH EXISTS, AND LIFE ALSO

SERGEY GOLOVIN never thought of death. It seemed to him something incidental and foreign. He was robust, endowed with that serenity in the joy of living which causes all evil thoughts, all thoughts fatal to life, to disappear rapidly, leaving the organism intact. Just as, with him, physical wounds healed quickly, so all injuries to his soul were immediately nullified. He brought into all his acts, into his pleasures and into his preparations for crime, the same happy and tranquil gravity: everything in life was gay, everything was important, worthy of being well done.

And he did everything well; he sailed a boat admirably, he was an excellent marksman. He was as faithful in friendship as in love, and had an unshakeable confidence in the "word of honor." His comrades declared laughingly that, if one who had been proved a spy should swear to Sergey that he was not a spy, Sergey would believe him and shake hands with him. A single fault: he thought himself a good singer, whereas he sang atrociously false, even in the case of revolutionary hymns. He got angry when they laughed at him.

"Either you are all asses, or else I am an ass!" he said

in a serious and offended tone. And, after a moment's re-
flection, the comrades declared, in a tone quite as serious:

"It is you who are an ass. You show it in your voice!"

And, as is sometimes the case with worthy people, they
loved him perhaps more for his eccentricities than for his
virtues.

He thought so little of death, he feared it so little, that
on the fatal morning, before leaving the dwelling of Tanya
Kovalchuk, he alone had breakfasted with appetite, as
usual. He had taken two glasses of tea, and eaten a whole
two-cent loaf. Then, looking with sadness at Werner's untouched bread, he said to him:

"Why don't you eat? Eat; it is necessary to get strength!"

"I am not hungry."

"Well, I will eat your bread! Shall I?"

"What an appetite you have, Sergey!"

By way of reply, Sergey, with his mouth full, began to
sing, in a false and hollow voice:

"A hostile wind is blowing o'er our heads."

After the arrest Sergey had a moment of sadness; the
plot had been badly planned. But he said to himself:
"Now there is something else that must be done well: to
die." And his gaiety returned. On his second day in the
fortress he began gymnastic exercises, according to the
extremely rational system of a German named Müller,
which interested him much. He undressed himself completely; and, to the amazement of the anxious sentinel, he
went carefully through the eighteen prescribed exercises.

As a propagander of the Müller system, it gave him much
satisfaction to see the soldier follow his movements. Although he knew that he would get no answer, he said to the
eye that appeared at the grating:

"That is the kind of thing that does you good, brother;
that gives you strength! That is what they ought to make
you do in the regiment," he added, in a gentle and per-
suasive voice, that he might not frighten the soldier, not
suspecting that his guardian took him for a madman.

The fear of death showed itself in him progressively,
seemingly by shocks: it seemed to him that someone was
thumping him violently in the heart from below. Then the
sensation disappeared, but came back a few hours later,
each time more intense and prolonged. It was beginning
already to take on the vague outlines of an unendurable
anguish.

"Is it possible that I am afraid?" thought Sergey, in
astonishment. "How stupid!"

It was not he who was afraid; it was his young, robust,
and vigorous body, which neither the gymnastics of Müller
nor the cold shower-baths could deceive. The stronger and
fresher he became after his cold-water ablutions, the more
acute and unendurable was his sensation of temporary fear.
And it was in the morning, after his deep sleep and physical
exercises, that this atrocious fear like something foreign
appeared—exactly at the moment when formerly he had
been particularly conscious of his strength and his joy in
living. He noticed this, and said to himself:

"You are stupid, my friend. In order that the body

may die more easily, it should be weakened, not fortified."

From that time he gave up his gymnastics and his massage. And, to explain this right-about-face, he cried to the soldier:

"Brother, the method is a good one. It is only for those who are going to be hanged that it is good for nothing."

In fact, he felt a sort of relief. He tried also to eat less in order to further weaken himself, but, in spite of the lack of air and exercise, his appetite remained excellent. Sergey could not resist it, and ate everything that they brought him. Then he resorted to a subterfuge; before sitting down to table, he poured half of his soup into his bucket. And this method succeeded; a great weariness, a vague numbness, took possession of him.

"I will teach you!" he said, threatening his body; and he caressed his softening muscles sadly.

But soon the body became accustomed to this régime and the fear of death appeared again, not in so acute a form, but as a vague sensation of nausea, still harder to bear. "It is because this lasts so long," thought Sergey. "If only I could sleep all the time until the day of execution!" He tried to sleep as much as possible. His first efforts were not altogether fruitless; then insomnia set in, accompanied with obsessing thoughts and, with these, a regret that he must part with life.

"Am I then afraid of it?" he asked himself, thinking of death. "It is the loss of life that I regret. Life is an admirable thing, whatever the pessimists may say. What would a pessimist say if they were to hang him? Ah! I regret to lose my life, I regret it much."

When he clearly understood that for him all was over, that he had before him only a few hours of empty waiting and then death, he had a queer feeling. It seemed to him that they had stripped him naked in an extraordinary fashion. Not only had they taken away his clothes, but also sun, air, sound and light, speech and the power of action. Death had not yet arrived, and yet life seemed already absent; he felt a strange sensation, sometimes incomprehensible, sometimes intelligible, but very subtle and mysterious.

"What is it then?" wondered Sergey, in his torment. "And I, where am I? I . . . What I?"

He examined himself attentively, with interest, beginning with his loose slippers, such as the prisoners wore, and stopping with his belly, over which hung his ample cloak. He began to walk back and forth in his cell, with arms apart, and continued to look at himself as a woman does when trying on a gown that is too long. He tried to turn his head: it turned. And what seemed to him a little terrifying was he himself, Sergey Golovin, who soon would be no more!

Everything became strange.

He tried to walk, and it seemed queer to him to walk. He tried to sit down, and he was surprised that he could do so. He tried to drink water, and it seemed queer to him to drink, to swallow, to hold the goblet, to see his fingers, his trembling fingers. He began to cough, and thought: "How curious it is! I cough."

"What is the matter? Am I going mad?" he asked himself. "That would be the last straw, indeed!"

He wiped his brow, and this gesture seemed to him equally surprising. Then he fixed himself in a motionless posture, without breathing—for entire hours, it seemed to him, extinguishing all thought, holding his breath, avoiding all motion; for every thought was madness, every gesture an aberration. Time disappeared as if transformed into space, into a transparent space in which there was no air, into an immense place containing everything—land and life and men. And one could take in everything at a glance, to the very extremity, to the edge of the unknown gulf, to death. And it was not because he saw death that Sergey suffered, but because he saw life and death at the same time. A sacrilegious hand had lifted the curtain which from all eternity had hidden the mystery of life and the mystery of death; they had ceased to be mysteries, but they were no more comprehensible than truth written in a foreign language.

"And here we are back to Müller again!" he suddenly declared aloud, in a voice of deep conviction. He shook his head and began to laugh gaily, sincerely:

"Ah, my good Müller! My dear Müller! My worthy German! You are right, after all, Müller; as for me, brother Müller, I am only an ass!"

He quickly made the round of his cell; and, to the great astonishment of the soldier who was watching him through the grating, he entirely undressed and went through the eighteen exercises with scrupulous exactness. He bent and straightened up his young body which had grown a little thin; he stooped, inhaling and exhaling the air; he raised himself on tiptoe, and moved his arms and legs.

"Yes, but, you know, Müller," reasoned Sergey, throwing out his chest, his ribs outlining themselves plainly under his thin, distended skin—"you know, Müller, there is still a nineteenth exercise—suspension by the neck in a fixed position. And that is called hanging. Do you understand, Müller? They take a living man, Sergey Golovin, for example, they wrap him up like a doll, and they hang him by the neck until he is dead. It is stupid, Müller, but that is the way it is; one must be resigned!"

He leaned on his right side, and repeated:

"One must be resigned, Müller!"

IX

THE HORRIBLE SOLITUDE

UNDER the same roof and to the same melodious chant of the indifferent hours, separated from Sergey and from Musya by a few empty cells, but as isolated as if he alone had existed in the whole universe, the unhappy Vasily Kashirin was finishing his life in anguish and terror.

Covered with sweat, his shirt adhering to his body, his formerly curly hair now falling in straight locks, he went back and forth in his cell with the jerky and lamentable gait of one suffering atrociously with the toothache. He sat down for a moment, and then began to run again; then he rested his forehead against the wall, stopped, and looked about as if in search of a remedy. He had so changed that one might think that he possessed two different faces, one of which, the younger, had gone nobody knows where, to give place to the second, a terrible face, that seemed to have come from darkness.

Fear had shown itself suddenly to him, and had seized upon his person as an exclusive and sovereign mistress. On the fatal morning, when he was marching to certain death, he had played with it; but that evening, confined in his cell, he had been carried away and lashed by a wave of mad terror. As long as he had gone freely forward to meet danger and death, as long as he had held his fate in his own hands, however terrible it might be, he had appeared tranquil and even joyous, the small amount of shameful and decrepit fear that he had felt having disappeared in a consciousness of infinite liberty, in the firm and audacious affirmation of his intrepid will, leaving no trace behind. With an infernal machine strapped around his waist, he had transformed himself into an instrument of death, he had borrowed from the dynamite its cruel reason and its flashing and homicidal power. In the street, among the busy people preoccupied with their affairs and quickly dodging the tramcars and the cabs, it seemed to him as if he came from another and an unknown world, where there was no such thing as death or fear.

Suddenly a brutal, bewildering change had taken place. Vasily no longer went where he wanted to go, but was led where others wanted him to go. He no longer chose his place; they placed him in a stone cage and locked him in, as if he were a thing. He could no longer choose between life and death; they led him to death, certainly and inevitably. He who had been for a moment the incarnation of will, of life, and of force, had become a lamentable specimen of impotence; he was nothing but an animal destined for the slaughter. Whatever he might say, they would not listen; if he started to cry out, they would stuff a rag in his mouth; and, if he even tried to walk, they would take him away and hang him. If he resisted, if he struggled, if he lay down on the ground, they would be stronger than he; they would pick him up, they would tie him, and thus they would carry him to the gallows. And his imagination gave to the men charged with this execution, men like himself, the new, extraordinary, and terrifying aspect of unthinking automata, whom nothing in the world could stop, and who seized a man, overpowered him, hanged him, pulled him by the feet, cut the rope, put the body in a coffin, carried it away, and buried it.

From the first day of his imprisonment, people and life had transformed themselves for him into an unspeakably frightful world filled with mechanical dolls. Almost mad with fear, he tried to fancy to himself that these people had tongues and spoke, but he did not succeed. Their mouths opened, something like a sound came from them; then they separated with movements of their legs, and all was over. He was in the situation of a man who, left alone in a house at night, should see all things become animate, move, and assume over him an unlimited power; suddenly the wardrobe, the chair, the sofa, the writing-table would sit in judgment upon him. He would cry out, call for help, beg, and rove from room to room; and the things would speak to each other in their own tongue; and then the wardrobe, the chair, the sofa, and the writing-table would start to hang him, the other things looking on.

In the eyes of Vasily Kashirin, sentenced to be hanged, everything took on a puerile aspect; the cell, the grated door, the striking apparatus of the clock, the fortress with its carefully modelled ceilings, and, above, the mechanical doll equipped with a musket, who walked up and down in the corridor, and the other dolls who frightened him by looking through the grating and handing him his food without a word.

A man had disappeared from the world.

In court the presence of the comrades had brought Kashirin back to himself. Again for a moment he saw people; they were there, judging him, speaking the language of men, listening, and seeming to understand. But, when he saw his mother, he felt clearly, with the terror of a man who is going mad and he knows it, that this old woman in a black neckerchief was a simple mechanical doll. He was astonished at not having suspected it before, and at having awaited this visit as something infinitely sorrowful in its distressing gentleness. While forcing himself to speak, he thought with a shudder:

"My God! But it is a doll! A doll-mother! And yonder is a doll-soldier; at home there is a doll-father, and this is the doll Vasily Kashirin."

When the mother began to weep, Vasily again saw something human in her, but this disappeared with the first words that she uttered. With curiosity and terror he watched the tears flow from the doll's eyes.

When his fear became intolerable, Vasily Kashirin tried to pray. There remained with him only a bitter, detestable, and enervating rancor against all the religious principles upon which his youth had been nourished, in the house of his father, a large merchant. He had no faith. But one day, in his childhood, he had heard some words that had made an impression upon him and that remained surrounded forever with a gentle poesy. These words were:

"Joy of all the afflicted!"

Sometimes, in painful moments, he whispered, without praying, without even accounting to himself for what he was doing: "Joy of all the afflicted!" And then he suddenly felt relieved; he had a desire to approach someone who was dear to him and complain gently:

"Our life! . . . but is it really a life? Say, my dear, is it really a life?"

And then suddenly he felt himself ridiculous; he would have liked to bare his breast and ask someone to beat it.

He had spoken to no one, not even to his best comrades, of his "Joy of all the afflicted!" He seemed to know nothing of it himself, so deeply hidden was it in his soul. And he evoked it rarely, with precaution.

Now that the fear of the unfathomable mystery which was rising before him completely covered him, as the water covers the plants on the bank when the tide is rising, he had a desire to pray. He wanted to fall upon his knees, but was seized with shame before the sentinel; so, with hands clasped upon his breast, he murmured in a low voice:

"Joy of all the afflicted!"

And he repeated with anxiety, in a tone of supplication: "Joy of all the afflicted, descend into me, sustain me!"

Something moved softly. It seemed to him that a sorrowful and gentle force hovered in the distance and then vanished, without illuminating the shades of the agony.

In the steeple the hour struck. The soldier yawned long and repeatedly.

"Joy of all the afflicted! You are silent! And you will say nothing to Vasily Kashirin!"

He wore an imploring smile, and waited. But in his soul there was the same void as around him. Useless and tormenting thoughts came to him; again he saw the lighted candles, the priest in his robe, the holy image painted on the wall, his father bending and straightening up again, praying and kneeling, casting furtive glances at Vasily to see if he too was praying or was simply amusing himself. And Kashirin was in still deeper anguish than before.

Everything disappeared.

His consciousness went out like the dying embers that one scatters on the hearth; it froze, like the body of a man just dead in which the heart is still warm while the hands and feet are already cold.

Vasily had a moment of wild terror when they came into his cell to get him. He did not even suspect that the hour of the execution had arrived; he simply saw the people and took fright, almost like a child.

"I will not do it again! I will not do it again!" he whispered, without being heard; and his lips became icy as he recoiled slowly toward the rear of his cell, just as in childhood he had tried to escape the punishments of his father.

"You will have to go . . ."

They talked, they walked around him, they gave him he knew not what. He closed his eyes, staggered, and began to prepare himself painfully. Undoubtedly he had recovered consciousness; he suddenly asked a cigarette of one of the officials, who amiably extended his cigarette-case.

X

THE WALLS CRUMBLE

THE unknown, surnamed Werner, was a man fatigued by struggle. He had loved life, the theatre, society, art, literature, passionately. Endowed with an excellent memory, he spoke several languages perfectly. He was fond of dress, and had excellent manners. Of the whole group of terrorists he was the only one who was able to appear in society without risk of recognition.

For a long time already, and without his comrades having noticed it, he had entertained a profound contempt for men. More of a mathematician than a poet, ecstasy and inspiration had remained so far things unknown to him; at times he would look upon himself as a madman seeking to square the circle in seas of human blood. The enemy against which he daily struggled could not inspire him with respect; it was nothing but a compact network of stupidities, treasons, falsehoods, base deceits. The thing that had finally destroyed in him forever, it seemed to him, the desire to live, was his execution of a police-spy in obedience to the order of his party. He had killed him tranquilly, but at sight of this human countenance, inanimate, calm, but still false, pitiable in spite of everything, he suddenly lost his esteem for himself and his work. He considered himself as the most indifferent, the least interesting, of beings. Being a man of will, he did not leave his party; apparently he remained the same; but from that time there was something cold and terrifying in his eyes. He said nothing to anyone.

He possessed also a very rare quality: he knew not fear. He pitied those of his comrades who had this feeling, especially Vasily Kashirin. But his pity was cold, almost official.

Werner understood that the execution was not simply death, but also something more. In any case, he was determined to meet it calmly, to live until the end as if nothing had happened or would happen. Only in this way could he express the profoundest contempt for the execution and preserve his liberty of mind. In the courtroom—his comrades, although knowing well his cold and haughty intrepidity, perhaps would not have believed it themselves —he thought not of life or of death: he played in his mind a difficult game of chess, giving it his deepest and quietest attention. An excellent player, he had begun this game on the very day of his imprisonment, and he kept it up continually. And the verdict that condemned him did not displace a single piece on the invisible board.

The idea that he probably would not finish the game did not stop Werner. On the morning of the last day he began by correcting a plan that had failed the night before. With hands pressed between his knees, he sat a long time motionless; then he arose, and began to walk, reflecting. He had a gait of his own; the upper part of his body inclined a little forward, and he brought down his heels forcibly; even when the ground was dry, he left clear foot-prints behind him. He whistled softly a rather simple Italian melody, which helped him to reflect.

But now he was shrugging his shoulders and feeling his pulse. His heart beat fast, but tranquilly and regularly, with a sonorous force. Like a novice thrown into prison for the first time, he examined attentively the cell, the bolts, the chair screwed to the wall, and said to himself:

"Why have I such a sensation of joy, of liberty? Yes, of liberty; I think of to-morrow's execution, and it seems to me that it does not exist. I look at the walls, and they seem to me not to exist either. And I feel as free as if instead of being in prison, I had just come out of another cell in which I had been confined all my life."

Werner's hands began to tremble, a thing unknown to him. His thought became more and more vibrant. It seemed to him that tongues of fire were moving in his head, trying to escape from his brain to lighten the still obscure dis-tance. Finally the flame darted forth, and the horizon was brilliantly illuminated.

The vague lassitude that had tortured Werner during the last two years had disappeared at the sight of death; his beautiful youth came back as he played. It was even something more than beautiful youth. With the astonish-ing clearness of mind that sometimes lifts man to the su-preme heights of meditation, Werner saw suddenly both life and death; and the majesty of this new spectacle struck him. He seemed to be following a path as narrow as the edge of a blade, on the crest of the loftiest mountain. On one side he saw life, and on the other he saw death; and they were like two deep seas, sparkling and beautiful, melting into each other at the horizon in a single infinite extension.

"What is this, then? What a divine spectacle!" said he slowly.

He arose involuntarily and straightened up, as if in presence of the Supreme Being. And, annihilating the walls, annihilating space and time, by the force of his all-penetrating look, he cast his eyes into the depths of the life that he had quitted.

And life took on a new aspect. He no longer tried, as of old, to translate into words what he was; moreover, in the whole range of human language, still so poor and miserly, he found no words adequate. The paltry, dirty, and evil things that suggested to him contempt and sometimes even disgust at the sight of men had completely disappeared, just as, to people rising in a balloon, the mud and filth of the narrow streets become invisible and ugliness changes into beauty.

With an unconscious movement Werner walked toward the table and leaned upon it with his right arm. Haughty and authoritarian by nature, he had never been seen in a prouder, freer, and more imperious attitude; never had his face worn such a look, never had he so lifted up his head, for at no previous time had he been as free and powerful as now, in this prison, on the eve of execution, at the threshold of death.

In his illuminated eyes men wore a new aspect, an unknown beauty and charm. He hovered above time, and never had this humanity, which only the night before was howling like a wild beast in the forests, appeared to him so young. What had heretofore seemed to him terrible, unpardonable, and base became suddenly touching and naïve, just as we cherish in the child the awkwardness of its behaviour, the incoherent stammerings in which its unconscious genius glimmers, its laughable errors and blunders, its cruel bruises.

"My dear friends!"

Werner smiled suddenly, and his attitude lost its haughty and imposing force. Again he became the prisoner suffering in his narrow cell, weary of seeing a curious eye steadily fixed upon him through the door. He sat down, but not in his usual stiff position, and looked at the walls and the gratings with a weak and gentle smile such as his face had never worn. And something happened which had never happened to him before: he wept.

"My dear comrades!" he whispered, shedding bitter tears. "My dear comrades!"

What mysterious path had he followed to pass from a feeling of unlimited and haughty liberty to this passionate and moving pity? He did not know. Did he really pity his comrades, or did his tears hide something more passionate, something really greater? His heart, which had suddenly revived and reblossomed, could not tell him. Werner wept, and whispered:

"My dear comrades! My dear comrades!"

And in this man who wept, and who smiled through his tears, no one—not the judges, or his comrades, or himself —would have recognized the cold and haughty Werner, skeptical and insolent.

XI

ON THE WAY TO THE GALLOWS

BEFORE getting into the vehicles, all five of the condemned were gathered in a large cold room with an arched ceiling, resembling an abandoned office or an unused reception-room. They were permitted to talk with each other.

Only Tanya Kovalchuk took immediate advantage of the permission. The others pressed in silence hands as cold as ice or as hot as fire; dumb, trying to avoid each other's gaze, they formed a confused and distracted group. Now that they were reunited, they seemed to be ashamed of what they had felt individually in the solitude. They were afraid to look at each other, afraid to show the new, special, somewhat embarrassing thing that they felt or suspected in each other.

Nevertheless, they did look, and, after a smile or two, all found themselves at ease, as before; no change revealed itself, or, if something had happened, all had taken an equal share in it, so that nothing special was noticeable in any one of them. All talked and moved in a queer and jerky fashion, impulsively, either too slowly or too quickly. Sometimes one of them quickly repeated the same words, or else failed to finish a phrase that he had begun or thought he had already spoken. But nothing of all this did they notice. All blinkingly examined the familiar objects without recognizing them, like people who have suddenly taken off their glasses. They often turned around quickly, as if someone were calling them from the rear. But they did not notice this. The cheeks and ears of Musya and Tanya were burning. At first Sergey was a little pale; he soon recovered, and appeared as usual.

Vasily alone attracted attention. Even in such a group he was extraordinary and dreadful. Werner was moved, and said in a low voice to Musya, with deep anxiety:

"What is the matter with him, Musya? Is it possible that he has . . . ? Really, we must speak to him."

Vasily looked at Werner from a distance, as if he had not recognized him; then he lowered his eyes.

"But, Vasily, what is the matter with your hair? What is the matter with you? It is nothing, brother, it will soon be over! We must control ourselves! We really must!"

Vasily did not break the silence. But, when they had already concluded that he would say absolutely nothing, there came a hollow, tardy, terribly distant reply, such as the grave might give up after a long appeal:

"But there is nothing the matter with me. I am in control of myself!"

He repeated:

"I am in control of myself!"

Werner was delighted.

"Good, good! You are a brave fellow! All is well!"

But, when his eyes met the dark and heavy gaze of

Vasily, he felt a momentary anguish, asking himself: "But whence does he look? whence does he speak?" In a tone of deep tenderness, he said:

"Vasily, do you hear? I love you much!"

"And I too, I love you much!" replied a tongue that moved painfully.

Suddenly Musya seized Werner by the arm, and, expressing her astonishment forcibly, like an actress on the stage, she said:

"Werner, what is the matter with you? You said: 'I love you'? You never said that to anyone before. And why is your face so sparkling and your voice so tender? What is it? What is it?"

And Werner, also in the manner of an actor dwelling upon his words, answered, as he pressed the young girl's hand:

"Yes, I love, now! Do not tell the others. I am ashamed of it, but I love my brothers passionately!"

Their eyes met and burst into flame: everything about them became extinct, just as all other lights pale in the fugitive flash of the lightning.

"Yes!" said Musya. "Yes, Werner!"

"Yes!" he answered. "Yes, Musya, yes!"

They had understood something and ratified it forever. With sparkling eyes and quick steps Werner moved on again in the direction of Sergey.

"Sergey!"

But it was Tonya Kovalchuk that answered. Full of

joy, almost weeping with maternal pride, she pulled Sergey violently by the sleeve.

"Just listen, Werner! I weep on his account. I torment myself, and he, he does gymnastics!"

"The Müller system?" asked Werner, with a smile.

Sergey, somewhat confused, knit his brows.

"You do wrong to laugh, Werner! I have absolutely convinced myself . . ."

Everybody began to laugh. Gaining strength and firmness from their mutual communion, they gradually became again what they used to be; they did not notice it, and thought that they were always the same. Suddenly Werner stopped laughing; with perfect gravity he said to Sergey:

"You are right, Sergey! You are perfectly right!"

"Understand this then!" rejoined Sergey, satisfied. "Of course we . . ."

Just then they were asked to get into the vehicles. The officials even had the amiability to allow them to place themselves in their own fashion, in pairs. In general, they were very amiable with them, even too much so; were they trying to give evidence of a little humanity, or to show that they were not responsible for what was taking place and that everything was happening of itself? It is impossible to say, but all those taking part were pale.

"Go with him, Musya!" said Werner, pointing the young girl to Vasily, who stood motionless.

"I understand!" she answered, nodding her head. "And you?"

"I? Tanya will go with Sergey, you with Vasily. As for me, I shall be alone! What matters it? I can stand it, you know!"

When they had reached the courtyard, the damp and slightly warm air fell softly upon their faces and eyes, cut their breathing, and penetrated their shivering bodies, purifying them. It was hard to believe that this stimulant was simply the wind, a spring wind, gentle and moist.

The astonishing spring night had a flavor of melted snow, of infinite space; it made the stones resound. Brisk and busy little drops of water fell rapidly, one after another, making a sonorous song. But, if one of them delayed a little or fell too soon, the song changed into a joyous splash, an animated confusion. Then a big drop fell heavily, and again the spring-like song began, rhythmical and sonorous. Above the city, higher than the walls of the fortress, was the pale halo formed by the electric lights.

Sergey Golovin heaved a deep sigh, and then held his breath, as if regretting to expel from his lungs air so pure and fresh.

"Have we had this fine weather long?" Werner inquired. "It is spring!"

"Only since yesterday!" they answered politely and promptly. "There have been many cold days."

One after another the black vehicles came up, took in two persons, and went away in the darkness, toward the spot where a lantern was swinging in the gateway. Around each vehicle were moving the gray outlines of soldiers;

their horses' shoes resounded loudly; often the beasts slipped on the wet snow.

When Werner bent to get into the vehicle, a gendarme said to him, in a vague way:

"There is another in there who *goes* with you!"

Werner was astonished.

"Who *goes* where? Ah! Yes! Another one! Who is it?"

The soldier said nothing. In a dark corner something small and motionless, but alive, lay rolled up; an open eye shone under an oblique ray of the lantern. As he sat down, Werner brushed against a knee with his foot.

"Pardon me, comrade!"

There was no answer. Not until the vehicle had started did the man ask hesitatingly, in bad Russian:

"Who are you?"

"My name is Werner, sentenced to be hanged for an attempt upon the life of XX. And you?"

"I am Yanson. . . . I must not be hanged. . . ."

In two hours they would be face to face with the great mystery as yet unsolved; in two hours they would leave life for death; thither both were going, and yet they became acquainted. Life and death were marching simultaneously on two different planes, and to the very end, even in the most laughable and most stupid details, life remained life.

"What did you do, Yanson?"

"I stuck a knife into my boss. I stole money."

From the sound of his voice it seemed as if Yanson were

asleep. Werner found his limp hand in the darkness, and pressed it. Yanson lazily withdrew it.

"You are afraid?" asked Werner.

"I do not want to be hanged."

They became silent. Again Werner found the Esthonian's hand, and pressed it tightly between his dry and burning palms. It remained motionless, but Yanson did not try again to release it.

They stifled in the cramped vehicle, whost musty smell mingled with the odors of the soldiers' uniform, of the muck-heap, and of wet leather. The breath of a young gendarme, redolent of garlic and bad tobacco, streamed continually into the face of Werner, who sat opposite. But the keen fresh air came in at the windows, and thanks to this the presence of spring was felt in the little moving box even more plainly than outside. The vehicle turned now to the right, now to the left; sometimes it seemed to turn around and go back. There were moments when it appeared to the prisoners as if they had been going in a circle for hours. At first the bluish electric light came in between the heavy lowered curtains; then suddenly, after a turn, darkness set in; it was from this that the travellers gathered that they had reached the suburbs and were approaching the station of S——. Sometimes, at a sudden turn, Werner's bent and living knee brushed in a friendly way against the bent and living knee of the gendarme, and it was hard to believe in the approaching execution.

"Where are we going?" asked Yanson, suddenly. The

continuous and prolonged shaking of the sombre vehicle gave him vertigo and a little nausea.

Werner answered, and pressed the Esthonian's hand more tightly than before. He would have liked to say specially friendly and kind words to this little sleeping man, whom already he loved more than anyone in the world.

"Dear friend! I think that you are in an uncomfortable position! Draw nearer to me!"

At first Yanson said nothing, but after a moment he replied:

"Thank you! I am comfortable! And you, they are going to hang you too?"

"Yes!" replied Werner, with an unlooked-for gaiety, almost laughing. He made a free-and-easy gesture, as if they were speaking of some futile and stupid prank that a band of affectionate practical jokers were trying to play upon them.

"You have a wife?" asked Yanson.

"No! A wife! I! No, I am alone!"

"So am I! I am alone."

Werner, too, was beginning to feel the vertigo. At times it seemed to him that he was on his way to some festivity. A queer thing; almost all those who were going to the execution had the same feeling; although a prey to fear and anguish, they rejoiced vaguely in the extraordinary thing that was about to happen. Reality became intoxicated on madness, and death, coupling with life, gave birth to phantoms.

"Here we are at last!" said Werner, gay and curious, when the vehicle stopped; and he leaped lightly to the ground. Not so with Yanson, who resisted, without saying a word, very lazily it seemed, and who refused to descend. He clung to the handle of the door; the gendarme loosened his weak fingers, and grasped his arm. Ivan caught at the corner, at the door, at the high wheel, but yielded at every intervention of the gendarme. He adhered to things rather than gripped them. And it was not necessary to use much force to loosen his grasp. In short, they prevailed over him.

As always at night, the station was dark, deserted, and inanimate. The passenger trains had already passed, and for the train that was waiting on the track for the prisoners there was no need of light or activity. Werner was seized with ennui. He was not afraid, he was not in distress, but he was bored; an immense, heavy, fatiguing ennui filled him with a desire to go away no matter where, lie down, and close his eyes. He stretched himself, and yawned repeatedly.

"If only they did these things more quickly!" said he, wearily.

Yanson said nothing, and shuddered.

When the condemned passed over the deserted platform surrounded with soldiers, on their way to the poorly-lighted railway carriages, Werner found himself placed beside Sergey Golovin. The latter designated something with his hand, and began to speak; his neighbor clearly understood only the word "lamp"; the rest of the phrase was lost in a weary and prolonged yawn.

"What did you say?" asked Werner, yawning also.

"The reflector . . . the lamp of the reflector is smoking," said Sergey.

Werner turned around. It was true; the glass shades were already black.

"Yes, it is smoking!"

Suddenly he thought: "What matters it to me whether the lamp is smoking, when . . . ?" Sergey undoubtedly had the same idea. He threw a quick glance at Werner, and turned away his head. But both stopped yawning.

All walked to the train without difficulty; Yanson alone had to be led. At first he stiffened his legs, and glued the soles of his feet to the platform; then he bent his knees. The entire weight of his body fell upon the arms of the policemen; his legs dragged like those of a drunken man; and the toes of his boots ground against the wooden platform. With a thousand difficulties, but in silence, they lifted him into the railway-carriage.

Vasily Kashirin himself walked unsupported; unconsciously he imitated the movements of his comrades. After mounting the steps of the carriage, he drew back; a policeman took him by the elbow to sustain him. Then Vasily began to tremble violently and uttered a piercing cry, pushing away the policeman!

"Aie!"

"Vasily, what is the matter with you?" asked Werner, rushing toward him.

Vasily kept silence, shivering the while. The policeman, vexed and even chagrined, explained:

"I wanted to sustain him, and he—he . . ."

"Come, Vasily, I will sustain you," said Werner.

He tried to take his comrade's arm. But the latter repulsed him, and cried louder than ever.

"Vasily, it is I, Werner!"

"I know! Don't touch me! I want to walk alone!"

And, still trembling, he entered the carriage and sat down in a corner. Werner leaned toward Musya, and asked in a low voice, designating Vasily with his eyes:

"Well, how are things with him?"

"Badly!" answered Musya, in a whisper. "He is already dead. Tell me, Werner, does death really exist?"

"I don't know, Musya; but I think not!" answered Werner in a serious and thoughtful tone.

"That is what I thought! And he? I suffered on his account during the whole ride; it seemed to me that I was travelling beside a dead man."

"I don't know, Musya. Perhaps death still exists for some. Later it will not exist at all. For me, for instance, death has existed, but now it exists no more."

The slightly pallid cheeks of Musya reddened.

"It has existed for you, Werner? For you?"

"Yes, but no more. As for you!"

They heard a sound at the door of the railway carriage; Michka the Tzigane entered spitting, breathing noisily, and making a racket with his boot-heels. He glanced about him, and stopped short.

"There is no room left, officer!" he declared to the fatigued and irritated policeman. "See to it that I travel comfortably, otherwise I will not go with you! Rather hang me right here, to the lamp-post! Oh, the scoundrels, what a carriage they have given me! Do you call this a carriage? The devil's guts, yes, but not a carriage!"

But suddenly he lowered his head, stretched out his neck, and advanced towards the other prisoners. From the frame of his bushy hair and beard his black eyes shot a savage, sharp, and rather crazy look.

"Oh, my God!" he cried; "so this is where we are! How do you do, sir!"

He sat down opposite Werner, holding out his hand; then, with a wink, he leaned over and swiftly passed his hand across his companion's neck:

"You too? Eh?"

"Yes!" smiled Werner.

"All?"

"All!"

"Oh! oh!" said the Tzigane, showing his teeth. He examined the other prisoners with a swift glance, which nevertheless dwelt longest on Musya and Yanson.

"On account of the Minister?"

"Yes. And you?"

"Oh, sir, my case is quite another story. I am not so distinguished! I, sir, am a brigand, an assassin. That makes no difference, sir; move up a little to make room for me; it is not my fault that they have put me in your company! In the other world there will be room for all."

He took the measure of all the prisoners with a watchful, distrustful, and savage gaze. But they looked at him without a word, seriously and even with evident compassion. Again he showed his teeth, and slapped Werner several times on the knee.

"So that is how it is, sir! As they say in the song:

"'Take care to make no sound, O forest of green oaks!'"

"Why do you call me sir, when all of us . . ."

"You are right!" acquiesced the Tzigane, with satisfaction. "Why should you be sir, since you are to be hanged beside me? There sits the real sir!"

He pointed his finger at the silent policeman.

"And your comrade yonder, he doesn't seem to be enjoying himself hugely!" he added, looking at Vasily. "Say there, you are afraid?"

"No!" answered a tongue that moved with difficulty.

"Well, then, don't be so disturbed; there is nothing to be ashamed of. It is only dogs that wag their tails and show their teeth when they are going to be hanged; you are a man. And this marionette, who is he? He certainly is not one of your crowd?"

His eyes danced incessantly; constantly, with a hissing sound, he spat out his abundant and sweetish saliva. Yanson, doubled up motionless in a corner, slightly shook the ears of his bald fur cap, but said nothing. Werner answered for him.

"He killed his employer."

"My God!" exclaimed the Tzigane, in astonishment. "How is it that they permit such birds as that to kill people?"

For a moment he looked at Musya stealthily; then suddenly he turned, and fixed his straight and piercing gaze upon her.

"Miss! Say there, Miss! what is the matter with you? Your cheeks are pink, and you are laughing! Look, she is really laughing! Look! Look!" And he seized Werner's knee with his hooked fingers.

Blushing and somewhat confused, Musya squarely returned the gaze of the attentive and savage eyes that questioned her. All kept silence.

The little cars bounced speedily along the narrow track. At every turn or grade-crossing the whistle blew, the engineer being afraid of crushing somebody. Was it not atrocious to think that so much care and effort, in short all human activity, was being expended in taking men to be hanged? The maddest thing in the world was being done with an air of simplicity and reasonableness. Cars were running; people were sitting in them as usual, travelling as people ordinarily travel. Then there would be a halt as usual: "Five minutes' stop."

And then would come death—eternity—the great mystery.

XII

THE ARRIVAL

THE train advanced rapidly.

Sergey Golovin remembered to have spent the summer, some years before, in a little country-house along this very line. He had often travelled the road by day and by night, and knew it well. Closing his eyes, he could fancy himself returning by the last train, after staying out late at night with friends.

"I shall arrive soon," thought he, straightening up: and his eyes met the dark grated window. Around him nothing stirred. Only the Tzigane kept on spitting, and his eyes ran the length of the car, seeming to touch the doors and the soldiers.

"It is cold," said Vasily Kashirin between his thin lips, which seemed frozen.

Tanya Kovalchuk bestirred herself in a maternal fashion: "Here's a very warm kerchief to wrap around your . . ."

"Neck?" asked Sergey, and he was frightened by his own question.

"What matters it, Vasya? Take it."

"Wrap yourself up. You will be warmer," added Werner.

He turned to Yanson, and asked him tenderly:

"And aren't you cold, too?"

"Werner, perhaps he wants to smoke. Comrade, do you want to smoke?" asked Musya. "We have some tobacco."

"Yes, I want to."

"Give him a cigarette, Sergey," said Werner.

But Sergey was already holding out his cigarette-case.

And all began to watch tenderly Yanson's clumsy fingers as they took the cigarette and struck the match, and the little curl of bluish smoke that issued from his mouth.

"Thank you," said Yanson. "It is good."

"How queer it is," said Sergey.

"How queer what is?" asked Werner.

"The cigarette," answered Sergey, unwilling to say all that he thought.

Yanson held the cigarette between his pale and living fingers. With astonishment he looked at it. And all fixed their gaze on this tiny bit of paper, on this little curl of smoke rising from the gray ashes.

The cigarette went out.

"It is out," said Tanya.

"Yes, it is out."

"The devil take it!" said Werner, looking anxiously at Yanson, whose hand, holding the cigarette, hung as if dead. Suddenly the Tzigane turned, placed his face close to Werner's, and, looking into the whites of his eyes, whispered:

"Suppose, sir, we were to attack the soldiers of the convoy? What do you think about it?"

"No," answered Werner.

"Why? It is better to die fighting. I will strike a blow they strike back, and I shall die without noticing it."

"No, it is not necessary," said Werner. And he turned to Yanson:

"Why don't you smoke?"

Yanson's dried-up face wrinkled pitifully, as if someone had pulled the threads that moved the creases in his face As in a nightmare, Yanson sobbed in a colorless voice, shedding no tears:

"I can't smoke. Ah! Ah! Ah! I must not be hanged Ah! Ah! Ah!"

Everybody turned toward him. Tanya, weeping copiously stroked his arms and readjusted his fur cap.

"My dear, my friend, don't cry, my friend! My poor friend!"

Suddenly the cars bumped into one another and began to slow up. The prisoners rose, but immediately sat down again.

"Here we are," said Sergey.

It was as if all the air had suddenly been pumped out of the car. It became difficult to breathe. Their swollen heart became heavy in their breasts, rose to their throats, beat desperately and their blood, in its terror, seemed to revolt Their eyes looked at the trembling floor, their ears listened to the slowly-turning wheels, which began to turn more slowly still, and gently stopped.

The train halted.

The prisoners were plunged into a strange stupor. They did not suffer. They seemed to live an unconscious life

Their corporeal being was absent; only its phantom moved about, voiceless but speaking, silent but walking. They went out. They arranged themselves in pairs, breathing in the fresh air of the woods. Like one in a dream, Yanson struggled awkwardly: they dragged him from the car.

"Are we to go on foot?" asked someone, almost gaily.

"It isn't far," answered a careless voice.

Without a word they advanced into the forest, along a damp and muddy road. Their feet slipped and sank into the snow, and their hands sometimes clung involuntarily to those of their comrades. Breathing with difficulty the soldiers marched in single file, on either side of the prisoners. An irritated voice complained:

"Could they not have cleared the road? It is difficult to advance."

A deferential voice answered:

"It was cleaned, Your Honour, but it is thawing. There is nothing to be done."

The prisoners began to recover their consciousness. Now they seemed to grasp the idea: "It is true, they could not clean the roads"; now it became obscured again, and there remained only the sense of smell, which perceived with singular keenness the strong and healthy odor of the forest; and now again all became very clear and comprehensible, the forest, and the night, and the road . . . and the certainty that very soon, in a minute, implacable death would lay its hands upon them. And little by little a whispering began:

"It is almost four o'clock."

"I told you so. We started too early."

"The sun rises at five."

"That's right, at five: we should have waited."

They halted in the twilight. Near by, behind the trees, whose huge shadows were waving on the ground, swung silently two lanterns. There the gallows had been erected.

"I have lost one of my rubbers," said Sergey.

"Well?" asked Werner, not understanding.

"I have lost it. I am cold."

"Where is Vasily?"

"I don't know. There he is."

Vasily was standing close by them, gloomy and motionless.

"Where is Musya?"

"Here I am. Is that you, Werner?"

They looked at each other, their eyes avoiding the silent and terrible significant swaying of the lanterns. At the left the thin forest seemed to be growing lighter. And beyond, something vast and gray and flat appeared, whence came a moist breeze.

"That is the sea," said Sergey, sucking in the damp air. "That is the sea."

Musya answered by a line from the song:

> "My love as broad as is the sea."

"What did you say, Musya?"

> "The shores of life cannot contain
> My love as broad as is the sea."

" 'My love as broad as is the sea,' " repeated Sergey, pensively.

" 'My love as broad as is the sea,' " echoed Werner. And suddenly he exclaimed in astonishment:

"Musya, my little Musya, how young you still are!"

Just then, close to Werner's ear, sounded the breathless and passionate voice of the Tzigane:

"Sir, sir, look at the forest. My God! What is all that? And yonder! The lanterns! My God, is that the scaffold?"

Werner looked at him. The convulsed features of the unfortunate man were frightful to see.

"We must say our farewells," said Tanya.

"Wait! They still have to read the sentence. Where is Yanson?"

Yanson lay stretched in the snow, surrounded by people. A strong smell of ammonia filled the air around him.

"Well, doctor, will you soon be through?" asked someone, impatiently.

"It's nothing. A fainting fit. Rub his ears with snow. He is better already. You can read."

The light of a dark lantern fell upon the paper and the ungloved white hands. Both paper and hands trembled. The voice also.

"Gentlemen, perhaps it is better not to read. You all know the sentence."

"Do not read!" answered Werner for all; and the light immediately went out.

The condemned refused also the services of the priest. Said the Tzigane:

"No nonsense, father; you will forgive me, they will hang me."

The broad dark silhouette of the priest took a few steps backward and disappeared. The day was breaking. The snow became whiter, the faces of the condemned darker, and the forest barer and sadder.

"Gentlemen, you will go in pairs, choosing your companion. But I beg you to make haste."

Werner pointed to Yanson, who now was standing again, sustained by two soldiers.

"I will go with him. You, Sergey, take Vasily. You go first."

"All right."

"I am going with you, Musya," said Tanya. "Come, let us kiss each other!"

Quickly they kissed all round. The Tzigane kissed forcibly; they felt his teeth. Yanson kissed gently and softly, with mouth half open. He did not seem to understand what he was doing. When Sergey and Kashirin had taken a few steps, the latter stopped suddenly, and in a loud voice, which seemed strange and unfamiliar, shouted:

"Good-bye, comrades."

"Good-bye, comrade," they answered him.

The two started off again. All was quiet. The lanterns behind the trees became motionless. They expected to hear a cry, a voice, some sound or other, but there as here all was calm.

"Oh! My God!" exclaimed someone hoarsely.

They turned around: it was the Tzigane, crying desperately:

"They are going to hang us."

He struggled, clutching the air with his hands, and cried again:

"God! Am I to be hanged alone? My God!"

His convulsive hands gripped the hand of Werner, and he continued:

"Sir, my dear sir, my good sir. You will come with me, won't you?"

Werner, his face drawn with sorrow, answered:

"I cannot; I am with Yanson."

"Oh! My God! then I shall be alone. Why? Why?"

Musya took a step toward him, and said softly:

"I will go with you."

The Tzigane drew back, and fixed his big swollen eyes upon her:

"Will you?"

"Yes."

"But you are so little! You are not afraid of me? No, I don't want you to. I will go alone."

"But I am not afraid of you."

The Tzigane grinned.

"Don't you know that I am a brigand? And you are willing to go with me? Think a moment. I shall not be angry if you refuse."

Musya was silent. And in the faint light of the dawn her face seemed to take on a luminous and mystic pallor. Suddenly she advanced rapidly toward the Tzigane, and, taking his head in her hands, kissed him vigorously. He took her by the shoulders, put her away a little, and then kissed her loudly on her cheeks and eyes.

The soldier nearest them stopped, opened his hands, and let his gun fall. But he did not stoop to pick it up. He stood still for a moment, then turned suddenly, and began to walk into the forest.

"Where are you going?" shouted his comrade, in a frightened voice. "Stay!"

But the other painfully endeavored to advance. Suddenly he clutched the air with his hands, and fell, face downward.

"Milksop, pick up your gun, or I will pick it up for you," cried the Tzigane, firmly. "You don't know your duty. Have you never seen a man die?"

Again the lantern swung. The turn of Werner and Yanson had come.

"Good-bye, sir!" said the Tzigane, in a loud voice. "We shall meet again in the other world. When you see me there, don't turn away from me."

"Good-bye!"

"I must not be hanged," said Yanson again, in a faint voice.

But Werner grasped his hand, and Yanson took a few steps. Then he was seen to sink into the snow. They bent over him, lifted him up, and carried him, while he weakly struggled in the soldiers' arms.

And again the yellow lanterns became motionless.

"And I, Musya? Am I then to go alone?" said Tanya, sadly. "We have lived together, and now . . ."

"Tanya, my good Tanya!"

The Tzigane hotly interrupted, holding Musya as if he feared that they might tear her from him.

"Miss," he cried, "you are able to go alone. You have a pure soul. You can go alone where you like. But I cannot. I am a bandit. I cannot go alone. 'Where are you going?' they will say to me, 'you who have killed, you who have stolen?' For I have stolen horses, too, Miss. And with her I shall be as if I were with an innocent child. Do you understand?"

"Yes, I understand. Go on then! Let me kiss you once more, Musya."

"Kiss each other! Kiss each other!" said the Tzigane. "You are women. You must say good-bye to each other."

Then came the turn of Musya and the Tzigane. The woman walked carefully, her feet slipping, lifting her skirts by force of habit. Holding her with a strong hand, and feeling the ground with his foot, the man accompanied her to death. The lights became motionless. Around Tanya all was tranquil again, and solitary. The soldiers, gray in the dawn's pale light, were silent.

"I am left alone," said Tanya. And she sighed. "Sergey is dead, Werner and Vasily are dead. And Musya is dying. I am alone. Soldiers, my little soldiers, you see, I am alone, alone . . ."

The sun appeared above the sea. . . .

They placed the bodies in boxes, and started off with them. With elongated necks, bulging eyes, and blue tongues protruding from their mouths, the dead retraced the road by which, living, they had come.

And the snow was still soft, and the air of the forest was still pure and balmy.

On the white road lay the black rubber that Sergey had lost. . . .

Thus it was that men greeted the rising sun.

THE END

THE RED LAUGH

The Red Laugh

PART I

FRAGMENT I

. . . HORROR and madness.

I felt it for the first time as we were marching along the road—marching incessantly for ten hours without stopping, never diminishing our step, never waiting to pick up those that had fallen, but leaving them to the enemy, that was moving behind us in a compact mass only three or four hours later effacing the marks of our feet by their own.

It was very sultry. I do not know how many degrees there were—120°, 140°, or more—I only know that the heat was incessant, hopelessly even and profound. The sun was so enormous, so fiery and terrible, that it seemed as if the earth had drawn nearer to it and would soon be burnt up altogether in its merciless rays. Our eyes had ceased to look. The small shrunk pupil, as small as a

poppy-seed, sought in vain for darkness under the closed
eyelid; the sun pierced the thin covering and penetrated
into the tortured brain in a blood-red glow. But, nevertheless, it was better so: with closed eyelids, and for a
long time, perhaps for several hours, I walked along with
my eyes shut, hearing the multitude moving around me:
the heavy, uneven tread of many feet, men's and horses,
the grinding of iron wheels, crushing the small stones,
somebody's deep strained breathing and the dry smack-
ing of parched lips. But I heard no word. All were
silent, as if an army of dumb people were moving, and
when anyone fell down, he fell in silence; others stumbled against his body, fell down and rose mutely, and,
without turning their heads, marched on, as though these
dumb men were also blind and deaf. I stumbled and fell
several times and then involuntarily opened my eyes, and
all that I saw seemed a wild fiction, the terrible raving
of a mad world. The air vibrated at a white-hot temperature, the stones seemed to be trembling silently, ready
to flow, and in the distance, at a curve of the road, the
files of men, guns and horses seemed detached from the
earth, and trembled like a mass of jelly in their onward
progress, and it seemed to me that they were not living
people that I saw before me, but an army of incorporate
shadows.

The enormous, near, terrible sun lit up thousands of
tiny blinding suns on every gun-barrel and metal plate,
and these suns, as fiery-white and sharp as the white-hot
points of the bayonets, crept into your eyes from every

side. And the consuming, burning heat penetrated into your body—into your very bones and brain—and at times it seemed to me that it was not a head that swayed upon my shoulders, but a strange and extraordinary globe, heavy and light, belonging to somebody else, and horrible.

And then—then I suddenly remembered my home: a corner of my room, a scrap of light-blue wall-paper, and a dusty untouched water-bottle on my table—on my table, which has one leg shorter than the others, and had a small piece of paper folded under it. While in the next room— and I cannot see them—are my wife and little son. If I had had the power to cry out, I would have done so—so wonderful was this simple and peaceful picture—the scrap of light-blue wall-paper and dusty untouched water-bottle. I know that I stood still and lifted up my arms, but somebody gave me a push from behind, and I quickly moved on, thrusting the crowd aside, and hastening whither I knew not, but feeling now neither heat nor fatigue. And I marched on thus for a long time through the endless mute files, past red sunburnt necks, almost touching the helplessly lowered hot bayonets, when suddenly the thought of what I was doing, whither I was hastening, stopped me. I turned aside in the same hasty way, forced my way to the open, clambered across a gulley and sat down on a stone in a preoccupied manner, as if that rough hot stone was the aim of all my strivings.

And then I felt it for the first time. I clearly perceived that all these people, marching silently on in the glaring sun, torpid from fatigue and heat, swaying and falling—

that they were all mad. They did not know whither they were going, they did not know what that sun was for, they did not know anything. It was not heads that they had on their shoulders, but strange and terrible globes. There— I saw a man in the same plight as I, pushing his way hurriedly through the rows and falling down; there—another, and a third. Suddenly a horse's head appeared above the throng with bloodshot and senseless eyes and a wide-open grinning mouth, that only hinted at a terrible unearthly cry; this head appeared, fell down, and for an instant the crowd stopped, growing denser in that spot; I could hear hoarse, hollow voices, then a shot, and again the silent endless march continued.

An hour passed as I sat on that stone, but the multitude still moved on past me, and the air and earth and the distant phantom-like ranks trembled as before. And again the burning heat pierced my body and I forgot what for an instant I had pictured to myself; and the multitudes moved on past me, but I did not know who they were. An hour ago I was alone on the stone, but now I was surrounded by a group of grey people; some lying motionless, perhaps dead; others were sitting up and staring vacantly at those passing by. Some had guns and resembled soldiers; others were stripped almost naked, and the skin on their bodies was so livid, that one did not care to look at it. Not far from me someone was lying with his bared back upturned.

One could see by the unconcerned manner in which he had buried his face in the sharp burning sand, by the whiteness of the palm of his upturned hand, that he was dead, but his back was as red as if he were alive, and only a slight yellowish tinge, such as one sees on smoked meat, spoke of death. I wanted to move away from him, but I had not the strength, and, tottering from weakness, I continued looking at the endless phantom-like swaying files of men. By the condition of my head I knew that I should soon have a sunstroke too, but I awaited it calmly, as in a dream, where death seems only a stage on the path of wonderful and confused visions.

And I saw a soldier part from the crowd and direct his steps in a decided manner towards us. For an instant I lost sight of him in a ditch, but when he reappeared and moved on towards us, his gait was unsteady, and in his endeavors to control his restlessly tossing body, one felt he was using his last strength. He was coming so straight upon me that I grew frightened and, breaking through the heavy torpor that enveloped my brain, I asked: "What do you want?"

He stopped short, as if it was only a word that he was waiting for, and stood before me, enormous, bearded, in a torn shirt. He had no gun, his trousers hung only by one button, and through a slit in them one could see his white body. He flung his arms and legs about and he was visibly trying to control them, but could not; the instant he brought his arms together, they fell apart again.

"What is the matter? You had better sit down," I said. But he continued standing, vainly trying to gather himself together, and stared at me in silence. Involuntarily I

got up from the stone and, tottering, looked into his eyes
—and saw an abyss of horror and insanity in them. Everybody's pupils were shrunk—but his had dilated and covered his whole eye: what a sea of fire he must have seen
through those enormous black windows! Maybe I had
only imagined it, maybe in his look there was only death
—but, no, I was not mistaken—in those black, bottomless
pupils, surrounded by a narrow orange-colored rim, like
a bird's eye, there was more than death, more than the
horror of death. "Go away!" I cried falling back. "Go
away!" And as if he was only waiting for a word, enormous, disorderly and mute as before, he suddenly fell down
upon me, knocking me over. With a shudder I freed my
legs from under him, jumped up and longed to run—somewhere away from men into the sunlit, unpeopled and quivering distance, when suddenly, on the left-hand side, a cannon
boomed forth from a hill-top, and directly after it two others,
like an echo. And somewhere above our heads a shell flew
past with a gladsome, many-voiced scr-e-e-ch and howl.

We were outflanked.

The murderous heat, fear and fatigue disappeared instantly. My thoughts cleared, my mind grew clear and sharp,
and when I ran up, out of breath, to the files of men
drawing up, I saw serene, almost joyous faces, heard hoarse,
but loud voices, orders, jokes. The sun seemed to have
drawn itself up higher so as not to be in the way, and had
grown dim and still—and again a shell, like a witch, cut
the air with a gladsome scr-e-e-ch.

I came up. . . .

FRAGMENT II

. . . . NEARLY all the horses and men. The same in the eighth battery. In our twelfth battery, towards the end of the third day, there remained only three guns—all the others being disabled—six men and one officer, myself. We had neither slept nor eaten for twenty hours; for three days and nights a Satanic roar and howl enveloped us in a cloud of insanity, isolated us from the earth, the sky and ourselves—and we, the living, wandered about like lunatics. The dead—they lay still, while we moved about doing our duty, talking and laughing, and we were—like lunatics. All our movements were quick and certain, our orders clear, the execution of them precise, but if you had suddenly asked any one of us who we were, undoubtedly we should not have been able to find an answer in our troubled brain. As in a dream all faces seemed familiar, and all that was going on seemed quite familiar and natural—as if it had happened before; but when I looked closely at any face or gun, or began listening to the din, I was struck by the novelty and endless mystery of everything. Night approached imperceptibly, and before we had time to notice it and wonder where it had come from, the sun was again burning above our heads. And only from those who came to our battery we learnt that it was the third day of the battle that was dawning, and instantly forgot it again: to us it appeared as one endless day without any beginning, sometimes dark, sometimes bright, but always incomprehensible and blind. And nobody was afraid of death, for nobody understood what death was.

On the third or fourth night—I do not remember which —I lay down for a minute behind the breastwork, and, as soon as I shut my eyes, the same familiar and extraordinary picture stood before them: the scrap of light-blue wall-paper and the dusty untouched water-bottle on my table. While in the next room—and I could not see them—were my wife and little son. But this time a lamp with a green shade was burning on the table, so it must have been evening or night. The picture stood motionless, and I contemplated it very calmly and attentively for a long time, letting my eyes rest on the light reflected in the crystal of the water-bottle, and on the wall-paper, and wondered why my son was not asleep: for it was night and time for him to go to bed. Then I again began examining the wall-paper: every spiral, silvery flower, square and line—and never imagined that I knew my room so well. Now and then I opened my eyes and saw the black sky with beautiful fiery stripes upon it, then shut them again and saw once more the wall-paper, the bright water-bottle, and wondered why my son was not asleep, for it was night and time for him to go to bed. Once a shell burst not far from me, making my legs give a jerk, and somebody cried out loudly, louder than the bursting of the shell, and I said to myself: "Somebody is killed," but I did not get up and did not tear my eyes away from the light-blue wall-paper and the water-bottle.

Afterwards I got up, moved about, gave orders, looked at the men's faces, trained the guns, and kept on wondering why my son was not asleep. Once I asked the sergeant, and he explained it to me at length with great detail, and we kept nodding our heads. And he laughed, and his left eyebrow kept twitching, while his eye winked cunningly at somebody behind us. Behind us were somebody's feet—and nothing more.

By this time it was quite light, when suddenly there fell a drop of rain. Rain—just the same as at home, the most ordinary little drops of rain. But it was so sudden and out of place, and we were so afraid of getting wet, that we left our guns, stopped firing, and tried to find shelter anywhere we could.

The sergeant with whom I had only just been speaking got under the gun-carriage and dozed off, although he might have been crushed any minute; the stout artilleryman, for some reason or other, began undressing a corpse, while I began running about the battery in search of something—a cloak or an umbrella. And the same instant over the whole enormous area, where the rain-cloud had burst, a wonderful stillness fell. A belated shrapnel-shot shrieked and burst, and everything grew still—so still that one could hear the stout artilleryman panting, and the drops of rain splashing upon the stones and guns. And this soft and continuous sound, that reminded one of autumn—the smell of the moist earth and the stillness—seemed to tear the bloody, savage nightmare asunder for an instant; and when I glanced at the wet, glistening gun it unexpectedly reminded me of something dear and peaceful—my childhood, or perhaps my first love. But in the distance a gun boomed forth particularly loud, and the spell of the momentary lull disappeared; the men began coming out of their hiding-places as suddenly as they had hid themselves; a gun roared, then another, and once again the weary brain was enveloped by bloody, indissoluble gloom. And nobody noticed when the rain stopped. I only remember seeing the water rolling off the fat, sunken yellow face of the killed artilleryman; so I supposed it rained for rather a long time. . . .

. . . . Before me stood a young volunteer holding his hand to his cap and reporting to me that the general wanted us to retain our position for only two hours more, when we should be relieved. I was wondering why my son was not in bed, and answered that I could hold on as much as he wished. But suddenly I became interested in the young man's face, probably because of its unusual and striking pallor. I never saw anything whiter than that face: even the dead have more colour than that young, beardless face had. I suppose he became terrified on his way to us, and could not recover himself; and in holding his hands to his cap he was only making an effort to drive away his mad fear by a simple and habitual gesture.

"Are you afraid?" I asked, touching his elbow. But his elbow seemed as if made of wood, and he only smiled and remained silent. Better to say, his lips alone were twitching into a smile, while his eyes were full of youth and terror only—nothing more.

"Are you afraid!" I repeated kindly. His lips twitched, trying to frame a word, and the same instant there hap-

pened something incomprehensible, monstrous and super-
natural. I felt a draught of warm air upon my right cheek
that made me sway—that is all—while before my eyes, in
place of the white face, there was something short, blunt
and red, and out of it the blood was gushing as out of an
uncorked bottle, such as is drawn on badly executed sign-
boards. And that short red and flowing "something" still
seemed to be smiling a sort of smile, a toothless laugh—a
red laugh.

I recognised it—that red laugh. I had been searching for
it, and I had found it—that red laugh. Now I understood
what there was in all those mutilated, torn, strange bodies.
It was a red laugh. It was in the sky, it was in the sun,
and soon it was going to overspread the whole earth—that
red laugh!

While they, with precision and calmness, like lunatics. . . .

FRAGMENT III

THEY say there are a great number of madmen in our
army as well as in the enemy's. Four lunatic wards have
been opened. When I was on the staff our adjutant showed
me. . . .

FRAGMENT IV

. . . Coiled round like snakes. He saw the wire, chopped through at one end, cut the air and coil itself round three soldiers. The barbs tore their uniforms and stuck into their bodies, and, shrieking, the soldiers spun round in frenzy, two of them dragging the third, who was already dead, after them. Then only one remained alive, and he tried to push the two that were dead away from him; but they trailed after him, whirling and rolling over each other and over him; and suddenly all three became motionless.

He told me that no less than two thousand men were lost at that one wire entanglement. While they were hacking at the wire and getting entangled in its serpentine coils, they were pelted by an incessant rain of balls and grapeshot. He assured me it was very terrifying, and if only they had known in which direction to run, that attack would have ended in a panic flight. But ten or twelve continuous lines of wire and the struggle with it, a whole labyrinth of pitfalls with stakes driven in at the bottom, had muddled them so, that they were quite incapable of defining the direction of escape.

Some, like men blind, fell into the funnel-shaped pits, and hung upon the sharp stakes, pierced through the stomach, twitching convulsively and dancing like toy clowns; they were crushed down by fresh bodies, and soon the whole pit filled to the edges, and presented a writhing mass of bleeding bodies, dead and living. Hands thrust themselves out of

it in all directions, the fingers working convulsively, catching
at everything; and those who once got caught in that trap
could not get back again: hundreds of fingers, strong and
blind, like the claws of a lobster, gripped them firmly by
the legs, caught at their clothes, threw them down upon
themselves, gouged out their eyes and throttled them. Many
seemed as if they were intoxicated, and ran straight at the
wire, got caught in it, and remained shrieking, until a bullet
finished them.

Generally speaking, they all seemed like people intoxicated: some swore dreadfully, others laughed when the
wire caught them by the arm or leg and died there and then.
He himself, although he had had nothing to eat or drink
since the morning, felt very queer. His head swam, and
there were moments when the feeling of terror in him
changed to wild rapture, and from rapture again to terror.
When somebody struck up a song at his side, he caught up
the tune, and soon a whole unanimous chorus broke forth.
He did not remember what they sang, only that it was lively
in a dancing strain. Yes, they sang, while all around them
was red with blood. The very sky seemed to be red, and
one could have thought that a catastrophe had overwhelmed
the universe—a strange disappearance of colors: the light-
blue and green and other habitual peaceful colors had disappeared, while the sun blazed forth in a red flare-light.

"The red laugh," said I.

But he did not understand.

"Yes, and they laughed, as I told you before, like people
intoxicated. Perhaps they even danced. There was some-

thing of the sort. At least the movements of those three resembled dancing."

He remembers distinctly, when he was shot through the chest and fell, his legs twitched for some time until he lost consciousness, as if he were dancing to music. And at the present moment, when he thinks of that attack, a strange feeling comes over him: partly fear and partly the desire to experience it all over again.

"And get another ball in your chest?" asked I.

"There now, why should I get a ball each time? But it would not be half so bad, old boy, to get a medal for bravery."

He was lying on his back with a waxen face, sharp nose, prominent cheek-bones and sunken eyes. He was lying looking like a corpse and dreaming of a medal! Mortification had already set in; he had a high temperature, and in three days' time he was to be thrown into the grave to join the dead; nevertheless he lay smiling dreamingly and talking about a medal.

"Have you telegraphed to your mother?" I asked.

He glanced at me with terror, animosity and anger, and did not answer. I was silent, and then the groans and ravings of the wounded became audible. But when I rose to go, he caught my hand in his hot, but still strong one, and fixed his sunken burning eyes upon me in a lost and distressed way.

"What does it all mean, ay? What does it all mean?" asked he in a frightened and persistent manner, pulling at my hand.

"What?"

"Everything . . . in general. Now, she is waiting for me. But I cannot. My country—is it possible to make her understand, what my country means?"

"The red laugh," answered I.

"Ah! you are always joking, but I am serious. It is indispensable to explain it; but is it possible to make her understand? If you only knew what she says in her letters! —what she writes. And you know her words—are grey-haired. And you—" he looked curiously at my head, pointed his finger and suddenly breaking into a laugh said: "Why, you have grown bald. Have you noticed it?"

"There are no looking-glasses here."

"Many have grown bald and grey. Look here, give me a looking-glass. Give me one! I feel white hair growing out of my head. Give me a looking-glass!" He became delirious, crying and shouting out, and I left the hospital.

That same evening we got up an entertainment—a sad and strange entertainment, at which, amongst the guests, the shadows of the dead assisted. We decided to gather in the evening and have tea, as if we were at home, at a picnic. We got a samovar, we even got a lemon and glasses, and established ourselves under a tree, as if we were at home, at a picnic. Our companions arrived noisily in twos and threes, talking, joking and full of gleeful expectation— but soon grew silent, and avoided looking at each other, for there was something fearful in this meeting of spared men. In tatters, dirty, itching, as if we were covered by a dreadful ringworm, with hair neglected, thin and worn, having lost all familiar and habitual aspect, we seemed to see each other for the first time as we gathered round the samovar, and seeing each other, we grew terrified. In vain I looked for a familiar face in this group of disconcerted men—I could not find one. These men, restless, hasty and jerky in their movements, starting at every sound, constantly looking for something behind their backs, trying to fill up that mysterious void into which they were too terrified to look, by superfluous gesticulations—were new, strange men, whom I did not know. And their voices sounded different, articulating the words with difficulty in jerks, easily passing into angry shouts or senseless irrepressible laughter at the slightest provocation. And everything around us was strange to us. The tree was strange, and the sunset strange, and the water strange, with a peculiar taste and smell, as if we had left the earth and entered into a new world together with the dead—a world of mysterious phenomena and ominous sombre shadows. The sunset was yellow and cold; black, unillumined, motionless clouds hung heavily over it, while the earth under it was black, and our faces in that ill-omened light seemed yellow, like the faces of the dead. We all sat watching the samovar, but it went out, its sides reflecting the yellowishness and menace of the sunset, and it seemed also an unfamiliar, dead and incomprehensible object.

"Where are we?" asked somebody, and uneasiness and fear sounded in his voice. Somebody sighed; somebody convulsively cracked his fingers; somebody laughed; somebody jumped up and began walking quickly round the table. These last days one could often meet with such men, who were always walking hastily, almost running, at times strangely silent, at times mumbling something in an uncanny way.

"At the war," answered he who had laughed, and again burst into a hollow, lingering laugh, as if something was choking him.

"What is he laughing at?" asked somebody indignantly. "Look here, stop it!"

The other choked once more, gave a titter and stopped obediently.

It was growing dark, the cloud seemed to be settling down on the earth, and we could with difficulty distinguish each other's yellow phantom-like faces. Somebody asked,—

"And where is Fatty-legs?"

"Fatty-legs" we called a fellow-officer, who, being short, wore enormous water-tight boots.

"He was here just now. Fatty-legs, where are you?"

"Fatty-legs, don't hide. We can smell your boots."

Everybody laughed, but their laugh was interrupted by a rough, indignant voice that sounded out of the darkness:

"Stop that! Are you not ashamed? Fatty-legs was killed this morning reconnoitring."

"He was here just now. It must be a mistake."

"You imagined it. Heigh-ho! you there, behind the samovar, cut me a slice of lemon."

"And me!"

"And me!"

"The lemon is finished."

"How is that, boys?" sounded a gentle, hurt voice, full

of distress and almost crying; "why, I only came for the sake of the lemon."

The other again burst into a hollow and lingering laugh, and nobody checked him. But he soon stopped. He gave a snigger, and was silent. Somebody said:

"To-morrow we begin the advance on the enemy."

But several voices cried out angrily:

"Nonsense, advance on the enemy, indeed!"

"But you know yourself——"

"Shut up. As if we cannot talk of something else."

The sunset faded. The cloud lifted, and it seemed to grow lighter; the faces became more familiar, and he, who kept circling round us, grew calmer and sat down.

"I wonder what it's like at home now?" asked he vaguely, and in his voice there sounded a guilty smile.

And once again all became terrible, incomprehensible and strange—so intensely so that we were filled with horror, almost to the verge of losing consciousness. And we all began talking and shouting at the same time, bustling about, moving our glasses, touching each other's shoulders, hands, knees—and all at once became silent, giving way before the incomprehensible.

"At home?" cried somebody out of the darkness. His voice was hoarse and quivering with emotion, fear and hatred. And some of the words would not come out, as if he had forgotten how to say them.

"At home? What home? Why, is there home anywhere? Don't interrupt me or else I shall fire. At home I used to take a bath every day—can you understand?—a bath with water—water up to the very edges. While now—I do not even wash my face every day. My head is covered with scurf, and my whole body itches and over it crawl, crawl . . . I am going mad from dirt, while you talk of—home! I am like an animal, I despise myself, I cannot recognise myself and death is not at all terrifying. You tear my brain with your shrapnel-shots. Aim at what you will, all hit my brain—and you can speak of—home. What home? Streets, windows, people, but I would not go into the street now for anything. I should be ashamed to. You brought a samovar here, but I was ashamed to look at it."

The other laughed again. Somebody called out:

"D—n it all! I shall go home."

"Home?"

"You don't understand what duty is!"

"Home? Listen! he wants to go home!"

There was a burst of laughter and of painful shouts—and again all became silent—giving way before the incomprehensible. And then not only I, but every one of us felt *that*. It was coming towards us out of those dark, mysterious and strange fields; it was rising from out of those obscure dark ravines, where, maybe, the forgotten and lost among the stones were still dying; it was flowing from the strange, unfamiliar sky. We stood around the dying-out samovar in silence, losing consciousness from horror, while an enormous, shapeless shadow that had risen above the world, looked down upon us from the sky with a steady and silent gaze. Suddenly, quite close to us, probably at the

Commanders' house, music burst forth, and the frenzied, joyous, loud sounds seemed to flash out into the night and stillness. The band played with frenzied mirth and defiance, hurriedly, discordantly, too loudly, and too joyously, and one could feel that those who were playing, and those who were listening, saw as we did, that same enormous, shapeless shadow, risen above the world. And it was clear the player on the trumpet carried in himself, in his very brain and ears, that same enormous dumb shadow. The abrupt and broken sound tossed about, jumping and running away from the others, quivering with horror and insanity in its lonesomeness. And the other sounds seemed to be looking round at it, so clumsily they ran, stumbling, falling, and again rising in a disorderly crowd—too loud, too joyous, too close to the black ravines, where most probably the forgotten and lost among the boulders were still dying.

And we stood for a long time around the cold samovar and were silent.

FRAGMENT V

. . . I was already asleep when the doctor roused me by pushing me cautiously. I woke, and jumping up, cried out, as we all did when anybody wakened us, and rushed to the entrance of our tent. But the doctor held me firmly by the arm, excusing himself:

"I frightened you, forgive me. I know you want to sleep . . ."

"Five days and nights . . ." I muttered, dozing off. I fell asleep and slept, as it seemed to me for a long time, when the doctor again began speaking, poking me cautiously in the ribs and legs.

"But it is very urgent. Dear fellow, please—it is so pressing. I keep thinking . . . I cannot . . . I keep thinking, that some of the wounded were left . . ."

"What wounded? Why, you were bringing them in the whole day long. Leave me in peace. It is not fair—I have not slept for five days!"

"Dear boy, don't be angry," muttered the doctor, awkwardly putting my cap on my head; "everybody is asleep, it's impossible to rouse anybody. I've got hold of an engine and seven carriages, but we're in want of men. I understand. . . . Dear fellow, I implore you. Everybody is asleep and everybody refuses. I'm afraid of falling asleep myself. I don't remember when I slept last. I believe I'm beginning to have hallucinations. There's a dear fellow, put down your feet, just one—there—there. . . ."

The doctor was pale and tottering, and one could see that if he were only to lie down for an instant he would fall asleep and remain so without waking for several days running. My legs sank under me, and I am certain I fell asleep as I walked—so suddenly and unexpectedly appeared before us a row of black outlines—the engine and carriages. Near them, scarcely distinguishable in the darkness, some men were wandering about slowly and silently.

There was not a single light either on the engine or carriages, and only the shut ash-box threw a dim reddish light on to the rails.

"What is this?" asked I, stepping back.

"Why, we are going in the train. Have you forgotten? We are going in the train," muttered the doctor.

The night was chilly and he was trembling from cold, and as I looked at him I felt the same rapid tickling shiver all over my body.

"D—n you!" I cried loudly. "Just as if you couldn't have taken somebody else."

"Hush! please, hush!" and the doctor caught me by the arm.

Somebody out of the darkness said:

"If you were to fire a volley from all the guns, nobody would stir. They are all asleep. One could go up and bind them all. Just now I passed quite close to the sentry. He looked at me and did not say a word, never stirred. I suppose he was asleep too. It's a wonder he does not fall down."

He who spoke yawned and his clothes rustled, evidently he was stretching himself. I leaned against the side of the carriage, intending to climb up—and was instantly overcome by sleep. Somebody lifted me up from behind and laid me down, while I began pushing him away with my feet, without knowing why, and again I fell asleep, hearing as in a dream fragments of a conversation:

"At the seventh verst."

"Have you forgotten the lanterns?"

"No, he won't go."

"Give them here. Back a little. That's it."

The carriages were jerking backwards and forwards, something was rattling. And gradually, because of all these sounds and because I was lying comfortably and quietly, sleep deserted me. But the doctor was sound asleep, and when I took him by the hand it was like the hand of a corpse, heavy and limp. The train was now moving slowly and cautiously, shaking slightly, as if groping its way. The student acting as hospital orderly lighted the candle in the lantern, lighting up the walls and the black aperture of the entrance, and said angrily:

"D—n it! Much they need us by this time. But you had better wake him, before he falls into a sound sleep, for then you won't be able to do anything with him. I know by myself."

We roused the doctor and he sat up, rolling his eyes vacantly. He tried to lie down again, but we did not let him.

"It would be good to have a drop of vodka now," said the student.

We drank a mouthful of brandy, and all sleepiness disappeared entirely. The big black square of the door began to grow pink, then red—somewhere from behind the hills appeared an enormous mute flare of a conflagration as if the sun was rising in the middle of the night.

"It's far away. About twenty versts."

"I feel cold," said the doctor, snapping his teeth.

The student looked out of the door and beckoned me to come up to him. I looked out: at different points of the horizon motionless flares of similar conflagration stood out in a mute row: as if dozens of suns were rising simultaneously. And now the darkness was not so great. The distant hills were growing more densely black, sharply outlined against the sky in a broken and wavy contour, while in the foreground all was flooded with a red soft glow, silent and motionless. I glanced at the student; his face was tinged by the same red fantastic color of blood, that had changed itself into air and light.

"Are there many wounded?" asked I.

He waved his hand.

"A great many madmen. More so than wounded."

"Real madmen?"

"What others can there be?"

He was looking at me, and his eyes wore the same fixed, wild expression, full of cold horror, that the soldier's had, who died of sunstroke.

"Stop that," said I, turning away.

"The doctor is mad also. Just look at him."

The doctor had not heard. He was sitting cross-legged, like a Turk, swaying to and fro, soundlessly moving his lips and finger-tips. And in his gaze there was the same fixed, stupefied, blunt, stricken expression.

"I feel cold," said he, and smiled.

"Hang you all!" cried I, moving away into a corner of the carriage. "What did you call me up for?"

Nobody answered. The student stood gazing out at the mute spreading glow, and the back of his head with its curly hair was youthful; and when I looked at him, I do not know why, but I kept picturing to myself a delicate woman's hand passing through that hair. And this image was so unpleasant, that a feeling of hatred sprang up in my breast, and I could not not look at him without a feeling of loathing.

"How old are you?" I asked, but he did not turn his head and did not answer.

The doctor kept on rocking himself.

"I feel cold."

"When I think," said the student, without turning round, "when I think that there are streets, houses, a University . . ."

He broke off, as if he had said all and was silent. Suddenly the train stopped almost instantaneously, making me knock myself against the wall, and voices were to be heard. We jumped out. In front of the very engine upon the rails lay something, a not very large lump, out of which a leg was projecting.

"Wounded?"

"No, dead. The head is torn off. Say what you will, but I will light the head-light. Otherwise we shall be crushing somebody."

The lump with the protruding leg was thrown aside; for an instant the leg lifted itself up, as if it wanted to run through the air, and all disappeared in a black ditch. The head-light was lit and the engine instantly grew black.

"Listen!" whispered somebody, full of silent terror.

How was it that we had not heard it before? From everywhere—the exact place could not be defined—a groan, unbroken and scraping, wonderfully calm in its breadth, and

even indifferent, as it seemed, was borne upon us. We
had heard many cries and groans, but this resembled none
of those heard before. On the dim reddish surface our
eyes could perceive nothing, and therefore the very earth
and sky, lit up by a never-rising sun, seemed to be groaning.

"The fifth verst," said the engine-driver.

"That is where it comes from," and the doctor pointed
forwards. The student shuddered, and slowly turned towards us.

"What is it? It's terrible to listen to!"

"Let's move on."

We walked along in front of the engine, throwing a
dense shadow upon the rails, but it was not black but of a
dim red color, lit up by the soft motionless flares, that
stood out mutely at the different points of the black sky.
And with each step we made, that wild unearthly groan,
that had no visible source, grew ominously, as if it was the
red air, the very earth and sky, that were groaning. In
its ceaselessness and strange indifference it recalled at times
the noise of grasshoppers in a meadow—the ceaseless noise
of grasshoppers in a meadow on a warm summer day. And
we came upon dead bodies oftener and oftener. We examined them rapidly, and threw them off the rails—those indifferent, calm, limp bodies, that left dark oily stains where
the blood had soaked into the earth where they had lain.
At first we counted them, but soon got muddled, and ceased.
They were many—too many for that ominous night, that
breathed cold and groans from each fibre of its being.

"What does it mean?" cried the doctor, and threatened somebody with his fist. "Just listen . . ."

We were nearing the sixth verst, and the groans were growing distinct and sharp, and we could almost feel the distorted mouths, from which those terrible sounds were issuing.

We looked anxiously into the rosy gloom, so deceitful in its fantastic light, when suddenly, almost at our feet, beside the rails, somebody gave a loud, calling, crying groan. We found him instantly, that wounded man, whose face seemed to consist only of two eyes, so big they appeared, when the light of the lantern fell on his face. He stopped groaning, and rested his eyes on each of us and our lanterns in turn, and in his glance there was a mad joy at seeing men and lights—and a mad fear that all would disappear like a vision. Perhaps he had seen men with lanterns bending over him many times, but they had always disappeared in a bloody confused nightmare.

We moved on, and almost instantly stumbled against two more wounded, one lying on the rails, the other groaning in a ditch. As we were picking them up, the doctor, trembling with anger, said to me: "Well?" and turned away. Several steps farther on we met a man wounded slightly, who was walking alone, supporting one arm with the other. He was walking with his head thrown back, straight towards us, but seemed not to notice us, when we drew aside to let him pass. I believe he did not see us. He stopped for an instant near the engine, turned aside, and went past the train.

"You had better get in!" cried the doctor, but he did not answer.

These were the first that we found, and they horrified us. But later on we came upon them oftener and oftener along the rails or near them, and the whole field, lit up by the motionless red flare of the conflagrations, began stirring as if it were alive, breaking out into loud cries, wails, curses and groans. All those dark mounds stirred and crawled about like half-dead lobsters let out of a basket, with outspread legs, scarcely resembling men in their broken, unconscious movements and ponderous immobility. Some were mute and obedient, others groaned, wailed, swore and showed such a passionate hate towards us who were saving them, as if *we* had brought about that bloody, indifferent night, and been the cause of all those terrible wounds and their loneliness amidst the night and dead bodies.

The train was full, and our clothes were saturated with blood, as if we had stood for a long time under a rain of blood, while the wounded were still being brought in, and the field, come to life, was stirring wildly as before.

Some of the wounded crawled up themselves, some walked up tottering and falling. One soldier almost ran up to us. His face was smashed, and only one eye remained, burning wildly and terribly, and he was almost naked, as if he had come from the bath-room. Pushing me aside, he caught sight of the doctor, and rapidly seized him by the chest with his left hand.

"I'll smash your snout!" he cried, shaking the doctor,

and added slowly and mordantly a coarse oath. "I'll smash your snouts, you rabble!"

The doctor broke away from the soldier, and advancing towards him, cried chokingly:

"I will have you court-martialled, you scoundrel! To prison with you! You're hindering my work! Scoundrel! Brute!"

We pulled them apart, but the soldier kept on crying out for a long time: "Rabble! I'll smash your snout!"

I was beginning to get exhausted, and went a little way off to have a smoke and rest a bit. The blood, dried to my hands, covered them like a pair of black gloves, making it difficult for me to bend my fingers, so that I kept dropping my cigarettes and matches. And when I succeeded in lighting my cigarette, the tobacco smoke struck me as novel and strange, with quite a peculiar taste, the like of which I never experienced before or after. Just then the ambulance student with whom I had travelled came up to me, and it seemed to me as if I had met with him several years back, but where I could not remember. His tread was firm as if he were marching, and he was staring through me at something farther on and higher up.

"And they are sleeping," said he, as it seemed, quite calmly.

I flew in a rage, as if the reproach was addressed to me.

"You forget, that they fought like lions for ten days."

"And they are sleeping," he repeated, looking through me and higher up. Then he stooped down to me and shak-

ing his finger, continued in the same dry and calm way:
"I will tell you—I will tell you . . ."

"What?"

He stooped still lower towards me, shaking his finger
meaningly, and kept repeating the words as if they ex-
pressed a completed idea:

"I will tell you—I will tell you. Tell them . . ." And
still looking at me in the same severe way, he shook his
finger once more, then took out his revolver and shot himself in the temple. And this did not surprise or terrify
me in the least. Putting my cigarette in the left hand, I felt
his wound with my fingers, and went back to the train.

"The student has shot himself. I believe he is still alive,"
said I to the doctor. The latter caught hold of his head
and groaned.

"D—n him! . . . There is no room. There, that one
will go and shoot himself, too, soon. And I give you my
word of honor," cried he, angrily and menacingly, "I will
do the same! Yes! And let me beg you—just walk back.
There is no room. You can lodge a complaint against me
if you like."

And he turned away, still shouting, while I went up to the
other who was about to commit suicide. He was an ambulance man, and also, I believe, a student. He stood, pressing
his forehead against the wall of the carriage, and his shoulders shook with sobs.

"Stop!" said I, touching his quivering shoulder. But he
did not turn round or answer, and continued crying. And
the back of his head was youthful, like the other student's,

and as terrifying, and he stood in an absurd manner with his legs spread out like a person drunk, who is sick; and his neck was covered with blood; probably he had clutched it with his own hands.

"Well?" said I, impatiently.

He pushed himself away from the carriage and, stooping like an old man, with his head bent down, he went away into the darkness away from all of us. I do not know why, but I followed him, and we walked along for a long time away from the carriages. I believe he was crying, and a feeling of distress stole over me, and I wanted to cry too.

"Stop!" I cried, standing still.

But he walked on, moving his feet ponderously, bent down, looking like an old man with his narrow shoulders and shuffling gait. And soon he disappeared in the reddish haze, that resembled light and yet lit nothing. And I remained alone. To the left of me a row of dim lights floated past—it was the train. I was alone—amidst the dead and dying. How many more remained? Near me all was still and dead, but farther on the field was stirring, as if it were alive—or so it seemed to me in my loneliness. But the moan did not grow less. It spread along the earth—high-pitched, hopeless, like the cry of a child or the yelping of thousands of cast-away puppies, starving and cold. Like a sharp, endless, icy needle it pierced your brain and slowly moved backwards and forwards—backwards and forwards. . . .

FRAGMENT VI

. . . THEY were our own men. During the strange confusion of all movements that reigned in both armies, our
own and the enemy's, during the last month, frustrating
all orders and plans, we were sure it was the enemy that
was approaching us, namely, the 4th corps. And everything was ready for an attack, when somebody clearly
discerned our uniforms, and ten minutes later our guess
had become a calm and happy certainty: they were our
own men. They apparently had recognized us too: they
advanced quite calmly, and that calm motion seemed to
express the same happy smile of an unexpected meeting.

And when they began firing, we did not understand for
some time what it meant, and still continued smiling—
under a hail of shrapnel and bullets, that poured down
upon us, snatching away at one stroke hundreds of men.
Somebody cried out by mistake and—I clearly remember
—we all saw that it was the enemy, that it was his uniform and not ours, and instantly answered the fire. About
fifteen minutes after the beginning of that strange engagement both my legs were torn off, and I recovered consciousness in the hospital after the amputation.

I asked how the battle had ended, and received an eva-
sive, reassuring answer, by which I could understand that
we had been beaten; and afterwards, legless as I was, I
was overcome by joy at the thought that now I would
be sent home, that I was alive—alive for a long time to

come, alive for ever. And only a week later I learnt
some particulars, that once more filled me with doubts
and a new, unexperienced feeling of terror. Yes, I believe they were our own men after all—and it was with
one of our shells, fired out of one of our guns by one of
our men, that my legs had been torn off. And nobody
could explain how it had happened. Something occurred,
something darkened our vision, and two regiments, belonging to the same army, facing each other at a distance of
one verst, had been destroying each other for a whole
hour in the full conviction that it was the enemy they had
before them. Later on the incident was remembered and
spoken of reluctantly in half-words and—what is most surprising of all—one could feel that many of the speakers
did not admit the mistake even then. That is to say, they
admitted it, but thought that it had occurred later on,
that in the beginning they really had the enemy before
them, but that he disappeared somewhere during the general fray, leaving us in the range of our own shells. Some
spoke of it openly, giving precise explanations, which
seemed to them plausible and clear. Up to this very minute I cannot say for certain how the strange blunder began,
as I saw with equal clearness first our red uniforms and
then their orange-colored ones. And somehow very soon
everybody forgot about the incident, forgot about it to
such an extent that it was spoken of as a real battle and
in that sense many accounts were written and sent to
the papers in all good faith; I read them when I was
back home. At first the public's attitude towards us, the

wounded in that engagement, was rather strange—we
seemed to be less pitied than those wounded in other battles, but soon even that disappeared too. And only new
facts, similar to the one just described, and a case in the
enemy's army, when two detachments actually destroyed
each other almost entirely, having come to a hand-to-hand
fight during the night—gives me the right to think that a
mistake did occur.

Our doctor, the one that did the amputation, a lean, bony
old man, tainted with tobacco smoke and carbolic acid, ever-
lastingly smiling at something through his yellowish-grey
thin mustache, said to me, winking his eye:

"You're in luck to be going home. There's something
wrong here."

"What is it?"

"Something's going wrong. In our time it was sim-
pler."

He had taken part in the last European war almost a
quarter of a century back and often referred to it with
pleasure. But this war he did not understand, and, as I
noticed, feared it.

"Yes, there's something wrong," sighed he, and frowned,
disappearing in a cloud of tobacco smoke. "I would leave
too, if I could."

And bending over me he whispered through his yellow
smoked mustache:

"A time will come when nobody will be able to go away
from here. Yes, neither I nor anybody," and in his old
eyes, so close to me, I saw the same fixed, dull, stricken

expression. And something terrible, unbearable, resembling the fall of thousands of buildings, darted through my head, and growing cold from terror, I whispered:

"The red laugh."

And he was the first to understand me. He hastily nodded his head and repeated:

"Yes. The red laugh."

He sat down quite close to me and looking round began whispering rapidly, in a senile way, wagging his sharp, grey little beard.

"You are leaving soon, and I will tell you. Did you ever see a fight in an asylum? No? Well, I saw one. And they fought like sane people. You understand—like sane people." He significantly repeated the last phrase several times.

"Well, and what of that?" asked I, also in a whisper, full of terror.

"Nothing. Like sane people."

"The red laugh," said I.

"They were separated by water being poured over them."

I remembered the rain that had frightened us so, and got angry.

"You are mad, doctor!"

"Not more than you. Not more than you in any case."

He hugged his sharp old knees and chuckled; and, looking at me over his shoulder and still with the echo of that unexpected painful laugh on his parched lips, he winked at me slyly several times, as if we two knew something very funny, that nobody else knew. Then with the solemnity of a professor of black magic giving a conjuring performance, he lifted his arm and, lowering it slowly, carefully touched with two fingers that part of the blanket under which my legs would have been, if they had not been cut off.

"And do you understand this?" he asked mysteriously.

Then, in the same solemn and significant manner, he waved his hand towards the row of beds on which the wounded were lying, and repeated:

"And can you explain this?"

"The wounded?" said I. "The wounded?"

"The wounded," repeated he, like an echo. "The wounded. Legless and armless, with pierced sides, smashed-in chests and torn-out eyes. You understand it? I am very glad. So I suppose you will understand this also?"

With an agility, quite unexpected for his age, he flung himself down and stood on his hands, balancing his legs in the air. His white working clothes turned down, his face grew purple and, looking at me fixedly with a strange upturned gaze, he threw at me with difficulty a few broken words:

"And this . . . do you . . . also . . . understand?"

"Stop!" whispered I in terror, "or else I will cry out."

He turned over into a natural position, sat down again near my bed, and, taking breath, remarked instinctively:

"And nobody can understand it."

"Yesterday they were firing again."

"Yes, they were firing yesterday and the day before," said he, nodding his head affirmatively.

"I want to go home!" said I in distress. "Doctor, dear fellow, I want to go home. I cannot remain here any longer. At times I cannot bring myself to believe that I have a home, where it is so good."

He was thinking of something and did not answer, and I began to cry.

"My God, I have no legs. I used to love my bicycle so, to walk and run, and now I have no legs. I used to dance my boy on the right foot and he laughed, and now . . . Curse you all! What shall I go home for? I am only thirty. . . . Curse you all!"

And I sobbed and sobbed, as I thought of my dear legs, my fleet, strong legs. Who took them away from me, who dared to take them away!

"Listen," said the doctor, looking aside. "Yesterday I saw a mad soldier that came to us. An enemy's soldier. He was stripped almost naked, beaten and scratched and hungry as an animal, his hair was unkempt, as ours is, and he resembled a savage, primitive man or monkey. He waved his arms about, made grimaces, sang and shouted and wanted to fight. He was fed and driven out again— into the open country. Where could we have kept him? Days and nights they wander about the hills, backwards and forwards in all directions, keeping to no path, having no aim or resting-place, all in tatters like ominous phantoms. They wave their arms, laugh, shout and sing, and when they come across anybody they begin to fight, or maybe, without noticing each other, pass by. What do they eat? Probably nothing, or, maybe, they feed on the dead bodies together with the beasts, together with those fat wild dogs, that fight in the hills and yelp the whole night long. At night they gather about the fires like monstrous moths or birds awakened by a storm, and you need only light a fire to have in less than half-an-hour a dozen noisy, tattered wild shapes, resembling chilled monkeys, gathering around it. Sometimes they are fired at by mistake, sometimes on purpose, for they make you lose all patience with their unintelligible, terrifying cries. . . ."

"I want to go home!" cried I, shutting my ears.

But new terrible words, sounding hollow and phantom-like, as if they were passing through a layer of wadding, kept hammering at my brain.

"They are many. They die by hundreds in the precipices and pitfalls, that are made for sound and clever men, in the remnants of the barbed wire and on the stakes they take part in the regular battles and fight like heroes—always in the foremost ranks, always undaunted, but often turn against their own men. I like them. At present I am only beginning to go mad, and that is why I am sitting and talking to you, but when my senses leave me entirely, I will go out into the open country—I will go out into the open country, and I will give a call—I will give a call, I will gather those brave ones, those knights-errant, around me, and declare war to the whole world. We will enter the towns and villages in a joyous crowd, with music and songs, leaving in our wake a trail of red, in which everything will whirl and dance like fire. Those that remain alive will join us, and our brave army will grow like an avalanche, and will cleanse the whole world. Who said that one must not kill, burn or rob? . . ."

He was shouting now, that mad doctor, and seemed to have awakened by his cries the slumbering pain of all those around him with their ripped-open chests and sides, torn-out eyes and cut-off legs. The ward filled with a broad, rasping, crying groan, and from all sides pale, yellow, exhausted faces, some eyeless, some so monstrously mutilated that it seemed as if they had returned from hell turned toward us. And they groaned and listened, and a black shapeless shadow, risen up from the earth, peeped in cautiously through the open door, while the mad doctor went on shouting, stretching out his arms.

"Who said one must not kill, burn, or rob? We will kill and burn and rob. We, a joyous careless band of braves, we will destroy all; their buildings, universities and museums, and merry as children, full of fiery laughter, we will dance on the ruins. I will proclaim the madhouse our fatherland; all those that have not gone mad—our enemies and madmen; and when I, great, unconquerable and joyous, will begin to reign over the whole world, its sole lord and master, what a glad laugh will ring over the whole universe."

"The red laugh!" cried I, interrupting him. "Help! Again I hear the red laugh!"

"Friends!" continued the doctor, addressing himself to the groaning, mutilated shadows. "Friends! we shall have a red moon and a red sun, and the animals will have a merry red coat, and we will skin all those that are too

white—that are too white. . . . You have not tasted blood?
It is slightly sticky and slightly warm, but it is red, and has
such a merry red laugh! . . ."

FRAGMENT VII

. . . It was godless and unlawful. The Red Cross is re-
spected by the whole world, as a thing sacred, and they
saw that it was a train full of harmless wounded and not
soldiers, and they ought to have warned us of the mine.
The poor fellows, they were dreaming of home. . . .

FRAGMENT VIII

. . . Around a samovar, around a real samovar, out of
which the steam was rising as out of an engine—the glass
on the lamp had even grown dim, there was so much steam.
And the cups were the same, blue outside and white inside,
very pretty little cups, a wedding present. My wife's sister
gave them—she is a very kind and good woman.

"Is it possible they are all whole?" asked I, incredulously, mixing the sugar in my glass with a clean silver spoon.

"One was broken," said my wife, absently; she was holding the tap open just then and the water was running out easily and prettily.

I laughed.

"What's it about?" asked my brother.

"Oh, nothing. Wheel me into the study just once more. You may as well trouble yourself for the sake of a hero. You idled away your time while I was away, but now that is over, I'll bring you to order," and I began singing, as a joke of course—"My friends, we're bravely hurrying towards the foe . . ."

They understood the joke and smiled, only my wife did not lift up her face, she was wiping the cups with a clean embroidered cloth. And in the study I saw once again the light-blue wall-paper, a lamp with a green shade and a table with a water-bottle upon it. And it was a little dusty.

"Pour me some water out of this," ordered I, merrily.

"But you've just had tea."

"That doesn't matter, pour me out some. And you," said I to my wife, "take our son, and go into the next room for a minute. Please."

And I drank the water with delight in small sips, while my wife and son were in the next room, and I could not see them.

"That's all right. Now come here. But why is he not in bed by this time?"

"He is so glad you have come home. Darling, go to your father."

But the child began to cry and hid himself at his mother's feet.

"Why is he crying?" asked I, in perplexity, and looked around, "why are you all so pale and silent, following me like shadows?"

My brother burst into a loud laugh and said, "We are not silent."

And my sister said, "We are talking the whole time."

"I will go and see about the supper," said my mother, and hurriedly left the room.

"Yes, you are silent," I repeated, with sudden conviction. "Since morning I have not heard a word from you; I am the only one who chats, laughs, and makes merry. Are you not glad to see me then? And why do you all avoid looking at me? Have I changed so? Yes, I am changed. But I do not see any looking-glasses about. Have you put them all away? Give me a looking-glass."

"I will bring you one directly," answered my wife, and did not come back for a long time, and the looking-glass was brought by the maid. I looked into it, and—I had seen myself before in the train, at the station—it was the same face, grown older a little, but the most ordinary face. While they, I believe, expected me to cry out and faint—so glad were they when I asked calmly—

"What is there so unusual in me?"

Laughing louder and louder, my sister left the room

hurriedly, and my brother said with calm assurance: "Yes, you have not changed much, only grown slightly bald."

"You can be thankful that my head is not broken," answered I, unconcernedly. "But where do they all disappear?—first one, then another. Wheel me about the rooms, please. What a comfortable armchair, it does not make the slightest sound. How much did it cost? You bet I won't spare the money; I will buy myself such a pair of legs, better . . . My bicycle!"

It was hanging on the wall, quite new, only the tires were limp for want of pumping. A tiny bit of mud had dried to the tire of the back wheel—the last time I had ridden it. My brother was silent and did not move my chair, and I understood his silence and irresoluteness.

"Only four officers remained alive in our regiment," said I, surlily. "I am very lucky. . . . You can take it for yourself—take it away to-morrow."

"All right, I will take it," agreed my brother submissively. "Yes, you are lucky. Half of the town is in mourning. While legs—that is really . . ."

"Of course I am not a postman."

My brother stopped suddenly and asked—"But why does your head shake?"

"That's nothing. The doctor said it will pass."

"And your hands too?"

"Yes, yes. And my hands too. It will all pass. Wheel me on, please. I am tired of remaining still."

They upset me, those discontented people, but my gladness returned to me when they began making my bed; a real bed, a handsome bed, that I had bought just before our wedding four years ago. They spread a clean sheet, then they shook the pillows and turned down the blanket; while I watched the solemn proceedings, my eyes were full of tears with laughing.

"And now undress me and put me to bed," said I to my wife. "How good it is!"

"This minute, dear."

"Quicker!"

"This minute, dear."

"Why; what are you doing?"

"This minute, dear."

She was standing behind my back, near the toilet table, and I vainly tried to turn my head so as to see her. And suddenly she gave a cry, such a cry as one hears only at the war—

"What does it all mean?"

She rushed towards me, put her arms round me, and fell down, hiding her head near the stumps of my cut-off legs, from which she turned away with horror, and again pressed herself against them, kissing them, and crying——

"What have you become? Why, you are only thirty years old. You were young and handsome. What does it all mean? How cruel men are. What is it for? For whom is it necessary? You, my gentle, poor darling, darling. . . ."

At her cry they all ran up—my mother, sister, nurse —and they all began crying and saying something or other, and fell at my feet wailing. While on the threshold stood

my brother, pale, terribly pale, with a trembling jaw, and
cried out in a high-pitched voice——

"I shall go mad with you all. I shall go mad!"

While my mother grovelled at my chair and had not
the strength to cry, but only gasped, beating her head
against the wheels. And there stood the clean bed with
the well-shaken pillows and turned-down blanket, the same
bed that I bought just before our wedding four years
ago. . . .

————

FRAGMENT IX

. . . I WAS sitting in a warm bath, while my brother was
pacing up and down the small room in a troubled manner,
sitting down, getting up again, catching hold of the soap and
towel, bringing them close up to his short-sighted eyes and
again putting them back in their places. At last he stood up
with his face to the wall and picking at the plaster with his
finger, continued hotly:

"Judge for yourself: one cannot teach people mercy,
sense, logic—teach them to act consciously for tens and
hundreds of years running with impunity. And, in particu-
lar, to act consciously. One can become merciless, lose all
sensitiveness, get accustomed to blood and tears and pain—
for instance butchers, and some doctors and officers do,
but how can one renounce truth, after one has learnt to

know it? In my opinion it is impossible. I was taught
from infancy not to torture animals and be compassionate;
all the books that I have read told me the same, and I am
painfully sorry for all those that suffer at your cursed
war. But time passes, and I am beginning to get accustomed to all those deaths, sufferings and all this blood; I
feel that I am getting less sensitive, less responsive in my
everyday life and respond only to great stimulants, but I
cannot get accustomed to *war;* my brain refuses to understand and explain a thing that is senseless in its basis.
Millions of people gather at one place and, giving their ac-
tions order and regularity, kill each other, and it hurts
everybody equally, and all are unhappy—what is it if not
madness?" My brother turned round and looked at me
inquiringly with his shortsighted, artless eyes.

"The red laugh," said I merrily, splashing about.

"I will tell you the truth," and my brother put his cold
hand trustingly on my shoulder, but quickly pulled it back,
as if he was frightened at its being naked and wet. "I
will tell you the truth; I am very much afraid of going
mad. I cannot understand what is happening. I cannot
understand it, and it is dreadful. If only anybody could
explain it to me, but nobody can. You were at the front,
you saw it all—explain it to me."

"Deuce take you," answered I jokingly, splashing about.

"There, and you too," said my brother sadly. "Nobody
is capable of helping me. It's dreadful. And I am beginning to lose all understanding of what is permissible and
what is not, what has sense and what is senseless. If I

were to seize you suddenly by the throat, at first gently, as if caressing you, and then firmly, and strangle you, what would that be?"

"You are talking nonsense. Nobody does such things."

My brother rubbed his cold hands, smiled softly, and continued:

"When you were away there were nights when I did not sleep, could not sleep, and strange ideas entered my head—to take a hatchet, for instance, and go and kill everybody—mother, sister, the servants, our dog. Of course they were only fancies, and I would never do so."

"I should hope not," smiled I, splashing about.

"Then again, I am afraid of knives, of all that is sharp and shining; it seems to me that if I were to take up a knife I should certainly kill somebody with it. Now, is it not true—why should I not plunge it into somebody; if it were sharp enough?"

"The argument is sufficient. What a queer fellow you are, brother! Just open the hot-water tap."

My brother opened the tap, let in some hot water, and continued:

"Then, again, I am afraid of crowds—of men, when many of them gather together. When of an evening I hear a noise in the street—a loud shout, for instance—I start and believe that . . . a massacre has begun. When several men stand together, and I cannot hear what they are talking about, it seems to me that they will suddenly cry out, fall upon each other, and blood will flow. And you know"—he bent mysteriously towards my ear—"the papers are full of murders—strange murders. It is all non-sense that there are as many brains as there are men; mankind has only one intellect, and it is beginning to get muddled. Just feel my head, how hot it is. It is on fire. And sometimes it gets cold, and everything freezes in it, grows benumbed, and changes into a terrible deadlike piece of ice. I must go mad; don't laugh, brother, I must go mad. A quarter of an hour has passed, it's time for you to get out of your bath."

"A little bit more. Just a minute."

It was so good to be sitting again in that bath and listening to the well-known voice, without reflecting upon the words, and to see all the familiar, simple and ordinary things around me: the brass, slightly-green tap, the walls, with the familiar pattern, and all the photographic outfit laid out in order upon the shelves. I would take up photography again, take simple, peaceful landscapes and portraits of my son walking, laughing and playing. One could do that without legs. And I would take up my writing again—about clever books, the progress of human thought, beauty, and peace.

"Ho, ho, ho!" roared I, splashing about.

"What is the matter with you?" asked my brother, growing pale and full of fear.

"Nothing. I am glad to be home."

He smiled at me as one smiles at a child or on one younger than oneself, although I was three years older than he, and grew thoughtful, like a grown-up person or an old man who has great, burdensome old thoughts.

"Where can one fly to?" he asked, shrugging his shoul-

ders. "Every day, at about the same hour, the papers close
the circuit, and all mankind gets a shock. This simul-
taneousness of feelings, tears, thoughts, sufferings and horror deprives me of all stay, and I am like a chip of wood
tossing about on the waves, or a bit of dust in a whirlwind.
I am forcibly torn away from all that is habitual, and there
is one terrible moment every morning, when I seem to hang
in the air over the black abyss of insanity. And I shall fall
into it, I must fall into it. You don't know all, brother.
You don't read the papers, and much is held back from you
—you don't know all, brother."

I took all his words for rather a gloomy joke—the usual
attitude towards all those who, being touched by insanity,
have an inkling of the insanity of war, and gave us a warning. I considered it as a joke, as if I had forgotten for the
moment, while I was splashing about in the hot water, all
that I had seen over there. "Well, let them hold things
back from me, but I must get out of the bath, anyway,"
said I lightly, and my brother smiled and called my man,
and together they lifted me out of my bath and dressed
me. Afterwards I had some fragrant tea, which I drank
out of my cut-glass tumbler, and said to myself that life
was worth living even without a pair of legs; and then they
wheeled me into the study up to my table and I prepared
for work.

Before the war I was on the staff of a journal review-
ing foreign literature, and now, disposed within my reach,
lay a heap of those dear, sweet books in yellow, blue and
brown covers. My joy was so great, my delight so pro-

found, that I could not make up my mind to begin reading them, and I merely fingered the books, passing my hand caressingly over them. I felt a smile spread over my face, most probably a very silly smile, but I could not keep it back, as I contemplated admiringly the type, the vignettes, the severe beautiful simplicity of the drawings. How much thought and sense of beauty there was in them all! How many people had to work and search, how much talent and taste were needed to bring forth that letter, for instance, so simple and elegant, so clever, harmonious and eloquent in its interlaced lines.

"And now I must set to work," said I, seriously, full of respect for work.

And I took up my pen to write the heading and, like a frog tied to a string, my hand began plunging about the paper. The pen stuck into the paper, scratched it, jerked about, slipped irresistibly aside, and brought forth hideous lines, broken, crooked, devoid of all sense. And I did not cry out or move, I grew cold and still as the approaching terrible truth dawned upon me; while my hand danced over the brightly illuminated paper, and each finger shook in such hopeless, living, insane horror, as if they, those fingers, were still at the front and saw the conflagrations and blood, and heard the groans and cries of undescribable pain. They had detached themselves from me, those madly quivering fingers, they were alive, they had become ears and eyes; and, growing cold from horror, without the strength to move or cry out, I watched their wild dance over the clean, bright white page.

And all was quiet. They thought I was working, and had shut all the doors, so as not to interrupt me by any sound—and I was alone in the room, deprived of the power of moving, obediently watching my shaking hands.

"It's nothing," said I aloud, and in the stillness and loneliness of the study my voice sounded hollow and nasty like the voice of a madman. "It is nothing. I will dictate. Why, Milton was blind when he wrote his *Paradise Regained.* I can think, and that is the chief thing, in fact it is all."

And I began inventing a long clever phrase about the blind Milton, but the words got confused, fell away as out of a rotten printing frame, and when I came to the end of the phrase I had forgotten the beginning. Then I tried to remember what made me begin, and why I was inventing that strange senseless phrase about Milton, and could not.

"Paradise Regained, Paradise Regained," I repeated, and could not understand what it meant.

And then I saw that I often forgot very many things, that I had become strangely absent-minded, and confused familiar faces; that I forgot words even in a simple conversation, and sometimes, remembering a word, I could not understand its meaning. And I clearly pictured to myself my daily existence. A strange short day, cut off like my legs, with empty mysterious spaces, long hours of unconsciousness or apathy, about which I could remember nothing.

I wanted to call my wife, but could not remember her name—and this did not surprise or frighten me. Softly I whispered:

"Wife!"

The incoherent, unusual word sounded softly and died away without bringing any response. And all was quiet. They were afraid of disturbing me at my work by any careless sound, and all was quiet—a perfect study for a savant —cosy, quiet, disposing one to meditation and creative energy. "Dear ones, how solicitous they are of me!" I thought tenderly.

. . . And inspiration, sacred inspiration, came to me. The sun burst forth in my head, and its burning creative rays darted over the whole world, dropping flowers and songs— flowers and songs. And I wrote on through the whole night, feeling no exhaustion, but soaring freely on the wings of mighty, sacred inspiration. I was writing something great —something immortal—flowers and songs—flowers and songs. . . .

PART II

FRAGMENT X

. . . Happily he died last week on Friday. I say "happily," and repeat that my brother's death was a great blessing to him. A cripple with no legs, palsied, with a smitten soul, he was terrible and piteous in his senseless creative ecstasy. Ever since that night he wrote for two months, without leaving his chair, refusing all food, weeping and scolding whenever we wheeled him away from his table even for a short time. He moved his dry pen over the paper with wonderful rapidity, throwing aside page after page, and kept on writing and writing. Sleep deserted him, and only twice did we succeed in putting him to bed for a few hours, thanks to a strong narcotic; but, later, even a narcotic was powerless to conquer his senseless creative ecstasy. At his order the curtains were kept drawn over all the windows the whole day long and the lamp was allowed to burn, giving the illusion of night, while he wrote on, smoking one cigarette after another. Apparently he was happy, and I never happened to meet any healthy person with such an inspired face—the face of a prophet or of a great poet. He became extremely emaciated, with the waxen transparency of a corpse or of an ascetic, and his hair grew quite grey; he began his senseless work a comparatively young man, but finished it an old one. Sometimes he hurried on his work, writing more than usual, and his pen would stick into the pages and break, but he never noticed it; at such times one durst not touch him, for at the slightest contact he was overtaken by fits of tears and laughter; but sometimes, very rarely, he rested blissfully from his work and talked to me affably, each time asking the same questions: Who was I, what was my name, and since when had I taken up literature.

And then he would condescendingly tell, always using the same words, what an absurd fright he had had at the thought that he had lost his memory and was incapable of work, and how splendidly he had refuted the insane supposition there and then by beginning his great immortal work about the flowers and songs.

"Of course I do not count upon being recognized by my contemporaries," he would say proudly and unassumingly at the same time, putting his trembling hand on the heap of empty sheets, "but the future—the future—will understand my idea."

He never once remembered the war or his wife and son; the mirage of his endless work engrossed his attention so undividedly that it is doubtful whether he was conscious of anything else. One could walk and talk in his presence—he noticed nothing, and not for an instant did his face lose its expression of terrible tension and inspiration. In the stillness of the night, when everybody was asleep and he alone wove untiringly the endless thread of insanity, he seemed terrible, and only his mother and

I ventured to approach him. Once I tried to give him a pencil instead of his dry pen, thinking that perhaps he really wrote something, but on the paper there remained only hideous lines, broken, crooked, devoid of any sense. And he died in the night at his work. I knew my brother well, and his insanity did not come as a surprise to me; the passionate dream of work that filled all his letters from the war and was the stay of his life after his return, had to come into inevitable collision with the impotence of his exhausted, tortured brain, and bring about the catastrophe. And I believe that I have succeeded in reconstructing with sufficient accuracy the successive feelings that brought him to the end during that fatal night. Generally speaking, all that I have written down concerning the war is founded upon the words of my dead brother, often so confused and incoherent; only a few separate episodes were burnt into his brain so deeply and indelibly that I could cite the very words that he used in telling me them. I loved him, and his death weighs upon me like a stone, oppressing my brain by its senselessness. It has added one more loop to the incomprehensible that envelops my head like a web, and has drawn it tight. The whole family has left for the country on a visit to some relatives, and I am alone in the house —the house that my brother loved so. The servants have been paid off, and only the porter from the next door comes every morning to light the fires, while the rest of the time I am alone, and resemble a fly caught between two window-frames,* plunging about and knocking myself against a

---

* In Russia the windows have double panes during the winter for the purpose of keeping out the cold.—Trans.

transparent but insurmountable obstacle. And I feel, I know, that I shall never leave the house. Now, when I am alone, the war possesses me wholly and stands before me like an inscrutable mystery, like a terrible spirit, to which I can give no form. I give it all sorts of shapes: of a headless skeleton on horseback, of a shapeless shadow, born in a black thundercloud mutely enveloping the earth, but not one of them can give me an answer and extinguish the cold, constant, blunt horror that possesses me.

I do not understand war, and I must go mad, like my brother, like the hundreds of men that are sent back from there. And this does not terrify me. The loss of reason seems to me honorable, like the death of a sentry at his post. But the expectancy, the slow and infallible approach of madness, the instantaneous feeling of something enormous falling into an abyss, the unbearable pain of tortured thought. . . . My heart has grown benumbed, it is dead, and there is no new life for it, but thought is still alive—still struggling, once mighty as Samson, but now helpless and weak as a child—and, I am sorry for my poor thought. There are moments when I cannot endure the torture of those iron clasps that are compressing my brain; I feel an irrepressible longing to run out into the street, into the market-place, where there are people and cry out:

"Stop the war this instant—or else . . ."

But what "else" is there? Are there any words that can make them come to their senses? Words, in answer to which one cannot find just such other loud and lying words? Or must I fall upon my knees before them and burst into tears? But then, hundreds of thousands are making the earth resound with their weeping, but does that change anything? Or, perhaps, kill myself before them all? Kill myself! Thousands are dying every day, but does that change anything?

And when I feel my impotence, I am seized with rage— the rage of war, which I hate. Like the doctor, I long to burn down their houses with all their treasures, their wives and children; to poison the water which they drink; to raise all the killed from their graves and throw the corpses into their unclean houses on to their beds. Let them sleep with them as with their wives or mistresses!

Oh, if only I were the Devil! I would transplant all the horrors that hell exhales on to their earth. I would become the lord of all their dreams, and, when they cross their children with a smile before falling asleep, I would rise up before them a black vision. . . . Yes, I must go mad—only let it come quicker—let it come quicker. . . .

FRAGMENT XI

. . . PRISONERS, a group of trembling, terrified men. When they were led out of the train the crowd gave a roar— the roar of an enormous savage dog, whose chain is too short and not strong enough. The crowd gave a roar and was silent, breathing deeply, while they advanced in a compact group with their hands in their pockets, smiling with their white lips as if currying favour, and stepping out in such a manner as if somebody was just going to strike them with a long stick under their knees from behind. But one of them walked at a short distance from the others, calm, serious, without a smile, and when my eyes met his black ones I saw bare open hatred in them. I saw clearly that he despised me and thought me capable of anything; if I were to begin killing him, unarmed as he was, he would not have cried out or tried to defend or right himself—he considered me capable of anything.

I ran along together with the crowd, to meet his gaze once more, and only succeeded as they were entering a house. He went in the last, letting his companions pass before him, and glanced at me once more. And then I saw such pain, such an abyss of horror and insanity in his big black eyes, as if I had looked into the most wretched soul on earth.

"Who is that with the eyes?" I asked of a soldier of the escort.

"An officer—a madman. There are many such."

"What is his name?"

"He does not say. And his countrymen don't know him. A stranger they picked up. He has been saved from hanging himself once already, but what is there to be done!" . . . and the soldier made a vague gesture and disappeared in the door.

And now, this evening I am thinking of him. He is alone amidst the enemy, who, in his opinion, are capable of doing anything with him, and his own people do not know him. He keeps silence and waits patiently for the moment when he will be able to go out of this world alto-gether. I do not believe that he is mad, and he is no coward; he was the only one who held himself with dignity in that group of trembling, terrified men, whom apparently he does not regard as his own people. What is he thinking about? What a depth of despair must be in the soul of that man, who, dying, does not wish to name himself. Why give his name? He has done with life and men, he has grasped their real value and notices none around him, either his own people or strangers, shout, rage and threaten as they will. I made inquiries about him. He was taken in the last terrible battle during which several tens of thousands of men lost their lives and he showed no resistance when he was being taken prisoner: he was unarmed for some reason or other, and, when the soldier, not having noticed it, struck him with his sword he did not get up or try to act in self-defence. But the wound, unhappily for him, was a slight one.

But, maybe, he is really mad? The soldier said there were many such. . . .

FRAGMENT XII

. . . IT IS beginning. When I entered my brother's study yesterday evening he was sitting in his armchair at his table heaped with books. The hallucination disappeared the moment I lighted a candle, but for a long time I could not bring myself to sit down in the armchair that he had occupied. At first it was terrifying—the empty rooms in which one was constantly hearing rustlings and crackings were the cause of this dread, but afterwards I even liked it—better he than somebody else. Nevertheless, I did not leave the armchair the whole evening; it seemed to me that if I were to get up he would instantly sit down in my place. And I left the room very quickly without looking round. The lamps ought to have been lit in all the rooms, but was it worth while? It would have been perhaps worse if I had seen anything by lamp-light—as it was, there was still room for doubt.

To-day I entered with a candle and there was nobody in the armchair. Evidently it must have been only a shadow. Again I went to the station—I go there every morning now—and saw a whole carriage full of our mad soldiers. It was not opened, but shunted on to another line, and I had time to see several faces through the windows. They were terrible, especially one. Fearfully drawn, the colour of a lemon, with an open black mouth and fixed eyes, it was so like a mask of horror that I could not tear my eyes away from it. And it stared at me, the whole of it, and was motionless, and glided past together with the moving carriage, just as motionless, without the slightest change, never transferring its gaze for an instant. If it were to appear before me this minute in that dark door, I do not believe I should be able to hold out. I made inquiries: there were twenty-two men. The infection is spreading. The papers are hushing up something and, I believe, there is something wrong in our town too. Black, closely-shut carriages have made their appearance—I counted six during one day in different parts of the town. I suppose I shall also go off in one of them one of these days.

And the papers clamour for fresh troops and more blood every day, and I am beginning to understand less and less what it all means. Yesterday I read an article full of suspicion, stating that there were many spies and traitors amongst the people, warning us to be cautious and mindful, and that the wrath of the people would not fail to find out the guilty. What guilty, and guilty of what? As I was returning from the station in the tram, I heard a strange conversation, I suppose in reference to the same article.

"They ought to be all hung without any trial," said one, looking scrutinisingly at me and all the passengers. "Traitors ought to be hung, yes."

"Without any mercy," confirmed the other. "They've been shown mercy enough!"

I jumped out of the tram. The war was making everybody shed tears, and they were crying too—why, what did it mean? A bloody mist seemed to have enveloped the earth, hiding it from our gaze, and I was beginning to think that the moment of the universal catastrophe was approaching. The red laugh that my brother saw. The madness was coming from over there, from those bloody burnt-out fields, and I felt its cold breath in the air. I am a strong man and have none of those illnesses that corrupt the body, bringing in their train the corruption of the brain also, but I see the infection catching me, and half of my thoughts belong to me no longer. It is worse than the plague and its horrors. One can hide from the plague, take measures, but how can one hide from all-penetrating thought, that knows neither distances nor obstacles?

In the daytime I can still fight against it, but during the night I become, as everybody else does, the slave of my dreams—and my dreams are terrible and full of madness. . . .

FRAGMENT XIII

. . . Universal mob-fights, senseless and sanguinary. The slightest provocation gives rise to the most savage club-law, knives, stones, logs of wood coming into action, and it is all the same who is being killed—red blood asks to be let loose, and flows willingly and plentifully.

There were six of them, all peasants, and they were

being led by three soldiers with loaded guns. In their quaint peasant's dress, simple and primitive like a savage's, with their quaint countenances, that seemed as if made of clay and adorned with felted wool instead of hair, in the streets of a rich town, under the escort of disciplined soldiers—they resembled slaves of the antique world. They were being led off to the war, and they moved along in obedience to the bayonets as innocent and dull as cattle led to the slaughter-house. In front walked a youth, tall, beardless, with a long goose neck, at the end of which was a motionless little head. His whole body was bent forward like a switch, and he stared at the ground under his feet as fixedly as if his gaze penetrated into the very depths of the earth. The last in the group was a man of small stature, bearded and middle-aged; he had no desire of resistance, and there was no thought in his eyes, but the earth attracted his feet, gripped them tightly, not letting them loose, and he advanced with his body thrown back, as if struggling against a strong wind. And at each step the soldier gave him a push with the butt-end of his rifle, and one leg, tearing itself from the earth, convulsively thrust itself forward, while the other still stuck tightly. The faces of the soldiers were weary and angry, and evidently they had been marching so for a long time; one felt they were tired and indifferent as to how they carried their guns and how they marched, keeping no step, with their feet turned in like countrymen. The senseless, lingering and silent resistance—of the peasants, seemed to have dimmed their disciplined brains, and they had ceased to understand where they were going and what their goal was.

"Where are you leading them to?" I asked of one of the soldiers. He started, glanced at me, and in the keen flash of his eyes I felt the bayonet as distinctly as if it were already at my breast.

"Go away!" said the soldier; "go away, or else . . ."

The middle-aged man took advantage of the moment and ran away; he ran with a light trot up to the iron railings of the boulevard and sat down on his heels, as if he were hiding. No animal would have acted so stupidly, so senselessly. But the soldier became savage. I saw him go close up to him, stoop down and, thrusting his gun into the left hand, strike something soft and flat with the right one. And then again. A crowd was gathering. Laughter and shouts were heard. . . .

FRAGMENT XIV

. . . In the eleventh row of stalls. Somebody's arms were pressing closely against me on my right- and left-hand side, while far around me in the semi-darkness stuck out motionless heads, tinged with red from the lights upon the stage. And gradually the mass of people, confined in that narrow space, filled me with horror. Everybody was silent, listening to what was being said on the stage or, perhaps, thinking out his own thoughts, but as they were many they were more audible, for all their silence, than the loud voices of the actors. They were coughing, blowing their noses, making a noise with their feet and clothes, and I could distinctly hear their deep, uneven breathing, that was heating the air. They were terrible, for each of them could become a corpse, and they all had senseless brains. In the calmness of those well-brushed heads, resting upon white, stiff collars, I felt a hurricane of madness ready to burst every second.

My hands grew cold as I thought how many and how terrible they were, and how far away I was from the entrance. They were calm, but what if I were to cry out "Fire!" . . . And full of terror, I experienced a painfully passionate desire, of which I cannot think without my hands growing cold and moist. Who could hinder me from crying out—yes, standing up, turning round and crying out: "Fire! Save yourselves—fire!"

A convulsive wave of madness would overwhelm their still limbs. They would jump up, yelling and howling like animals; they would forget that they had wives, sisters, mothers, and would begin casting themselves about like men stricken with sudden blindness, in their madness throttling each other with their white fingers fragrant with scent. The light would be turned on, and somebody with an ashen face would appear upon the stage, shouting that all was in order and that there was no fire, and the music, trembling and halting, would begin playing something wildly merry—but they would be deaf to everything—they would be throttling, trampling, and beating the heads of the women, demolishing their ingenious, cunning headdresses. They would tear at each other's ears, bite off each other's noses, and tear the very clothes off each other's bodies, feeling no shame, for they would be mad. Their sensitive, delicate, beautiful, adorable women would scream and writhe helplessly at their feet, clasping their knees, still believing in their generosity—while they would beat them viciously upon their beautiful upturned faces, trying to force their way towards the entrance. For men are always murderers, and their calmness and generosity is the calmness of a well-fed animal, that knows itself out of danger.

And when, having made corpses of half their number, they would gather at the entrance in a trembling, tattered group of shamefaced animals, with a false smile upon their lips, I would go on the stage and say with a laugh:

"It has all happened because you killed my brother." Yes, I would say with a laugh: "It has all happened because you killed my brother."

I must have whsipered something aloud, for my neighbor on the right-hand side moved angrily in his chair and said:

"Hush! You are interrupting."

I felt merry and wanted to play a joke. Assuming a warning severe expression, I stooped towards him.

"What is it?" he asked suspiciously. "Why do you look at me so?"

"Hush, I implore you," whispered I with my lips. "Do

you not perceive a smell of burning? There is a fire in the theatre."

He had enough power of will and good sense not to cry out. His face grew pale, his eyes starting out of their sockets and almost protruding over his cheeks, enormous as bladders, but he did not cry out. He rose quietly and, without even thanking me, walked totteringly towards the entrance, convulsively keeping back his steps. He was afraid of the others guessing about the fire and preventing him getting away—him, the only one worthy of being saved.

I felt disgusted and left the theatre also; besides I did not want to make known my *incognito* too soon. In the street I looked towards that part of the sky where the war was raging; everything was calm, and the night clouds, yellow from the lights of the town, were slowly and calmly drifting past.

"Perhaps it is only a dream, and there is no war?" thought I, deceived by the stillness of the sky and town.

But a boy sprang out from behind a corner, crying joyously:

"A terrible battle. Enormous losses. Buy a list of telegrams—night telegrams!"

I read it by the light of the street lamp. Four thousand dead. In the theatre, I should say, there were not more than one thousand. And the whole way home I kept repeating —"Four thousand dead."

Now I am afraid of returning to my empty house. When I put my key into the lock and look at the dumb, flat door, I can feel all its dark empty rooms behind it, which, however, the next minute, a man in a hat would pass through, looking furtively around him. I know the way well, but on the stairs I begin lighting match after match, until I find a candle. I never enter my brother's study, and it is locked with all that it contains. And I sleep in the dining-room, whither I have shifted altogether; there I feel calmer, for the air seems to have still retained the traces of talking and laughing, and the merry clang of dishes. Sometimes I distinctly hear the scraping of a dry pen—and when I lie down on my bed . . .

FRAGMENT XV

. . . THAT absurd and terrible dream. It seemed as if the skull had been taken off my brain and, bared and unprotected, it submissively and greedily imbibed all the horrors of those bloody and senseless days. I was lying curled up, occupying only five feet of space, while my thought embraced the whole world. I saw with the eyes of all mankind, and listened with its ears; I died with the killed, sorrowed and wept with all that were wounded and left behind, and, when blood flowed out of anybody's body, I felt the pain of the wound and suffered. Even all that had not happened and was far away, I saw as clearly as if it had happened and was close by, and there was no end to the sufferings of my bared brain.

Those children, those innocent little children. I saw them in the street playing at war and chasing each other, and one of them was already crying in a high-pitched, childish voice—and something shrank within me from horror and disgust. And I went home; night came on—and in fiery dreams, resembling midnight conflagrations, those innocent little children changed into a band of child-murderers.

Something was ominously burning in a broad red glare, and in the smoke there swarmed monstrous, misshapen children, with heads of grown-up murderers. They were jumping lightly and nimbly, like young goats at play, and were breathing with difficulty, like sick people. Their mouths, resembling the jaws of toads or frogs, opened widely and convulsively; behind the transparent skin of their naked bodies the red blood was coursing angrily—and they were killing each other at play. They were the most terrible of all that I had seen, for they were little and could penetrate everywhere.

I was looking out of the window and one of the little ones noticed me, smiled, and with his eyes asked me to let him in.

"I want to go to you," he said.

"You will kill me."

"I want to go to you," he said, growing suddenly pale, and began scrambling up the white wall like a rat—just like a hungry rat. He kept losing his footing, and squealed and darted about the wall with such rapidity that I could not follow his impetuous, sudden movements.

"He can crawl in under the door," said I to myself with horror, and as if he had guessed my thoughts, he grew thin and long and, waving the end of his tail rapidly, he crawled into the dark crack under the front door. But I had time to hide myself under the blanket, and heard him searching for me in the dark rooms, cautiously stepping along with his tiny bare foot. He approached my room very slowly, stopping now and then, and at last entered it; but I did not hear any sound, either rustle or movement, for a long time, as if there was nobody near my bed. And then somebody's little hand began lifting up the edge of the coverlet, and I could feel the cold air of the room upon my face and chest. I held the blanket tightly, but it persisted in lifting itself up on all sides; and all of a sudden my feet became so cold, as if I had dipped them into water. Now they are lying unprotected in the chill darkness of the room, and he was looking at them.

In the yard, behind the house, a dog barked and was silent, and I heard the trail of the chain as it went into its kennel. But he still watched my naked feet and kept silence; I knew he was there by the unendurable horror that was binding me like death with a stony, sepulchral immobility. If I could have cried out, I would have awakened the whole town, the whole world, but my voice was dead within me, and I lay submissive and motionless, feeling the little cold hands moving over my body and nearing my throat.

"I cannot!" I groaned, gasping and waking up for an

instant, I saw the vigilant darkness of the night, mysterious and living, and again I believe I fell asleep. . . .

"Don't fear," said my brother, sitting down upon my bed, and the bed creaked, so heavy was he—dead. "Never fear, you see it is a dream. You only imagine that you were being strangled, while in reality you are asleep in the dark rooms, where there is not a soul, and I am in my study writing. Nobody understood what I wrote about, and you derided me as one insane, but now I will tell you the truth. I am writing about the red laugh. Do you see it?"

Something enormous, red and bloody, was standing before me, laughing a toothless laugh.

"That is the red laugh. When the earth goes mad, it begins to laugh like that. You know, the earth has gone mad. There are no more flowers or songs on it; it has become round, smooth and red like a scalped head. Do you see it?"

"Yes, I see it. It is laughing."

"Look what its brain is like. It is red, like bloody porridge, and is muddled."

"It is crying out."

"It is in pain. It has no flowers or songs. And now— let me lie down upon you."

"You are heavy and I am afraid."

"We, the dead, lie down on the living. Do you feel warm?"

"Yes."

"Are you comfortable?"

"I am dying."

"Awake and cry out. Awake and cry out. I am going away. . . ."

FRAGMENT XVI

. . . To-day is the eighth day of the battle. It began last Friday, and Saturday, Sunday, Monday, Tuesday, Wednesday and Thursday have passed—and Friday has come again and is gone—and it is still going on. Both armies, hundreds of thousands of men, are standing in front of each other, never flinching, sending explosive, crashing projectiles without stopping, and every instant living men are turned into corpses. The roar and incessant vibration of the air has made the very sky shudder and gather black thunderclouds above their heads—while they continue to stand in front of each other, never flinching and still killing each other. If a man does not sleep for three nights, he becomes ill and loses his memory, but they have not slept for a whole week, and are all mad. That is why they feel no pain, do not retreat, and go on fighting until they have killed all to the last man. They say that some of the detachments came to the end of their ammunition, but still they fought on, using their fists and stones, and biting each other like dogs. If the remnants of those regiments return home, they will have canine teeth like wolves—but they will not return, they have gone mad and die, every man of them. They have gone mad. Everything is mud-

dled in their heads, and they cease to understand anything!
If they were to be turned round suddenly and sharply, they
would begin firing at their own men, thinking that they
were firing at the enemy.

Strange rumours—strange rumours that are told in a
whisper, those repeating them turning white from horror
and dreadful forebodings. Brother, brother, listen what is
being told of the red laugh! They say phantom regiments
have appeared, large bands of shadows, the exact copy of
living men. At night, when the men forget themselves for
an instant in sleep, or in the thick of the day's fight, when
the bright day itself seems a phantom, they suddenly appear, firing out of phantom guns, filling the air with phantom noises; and men, living but insane men, astounded by
the suddenness of the attack, fight to the death against
the phantom enemy, go mad from horror, become grey in
an instant and die. The phantoms disappear as suddenly
as they appear, and all becomes still, while the earth is
strewn with fresh mutilated bodies. Who killed them? You
know, brother, who killed them. When there is a lull
between two battles and the enemy is far off, suddenly
in the darkness of the night there resounds a solitary,
frightened shot. And all jump up and begin firing into the
darkness, into the silent dumb darkness, for a long time,
for whole hours. Whom do they see there? Whose terrible,
silent shape, full of horror and madness appears before
them? You know, brother, and I know, but men do not
know yet, but they have a foreboding, and ask, turning pale:

"Why are there so many madmen? Before there never used to be so many."

"Before there never used to be so many madmen," they say, turning pale, trying to believe that now it is as before, and that the universal violence done to the brains of humanity would have no effect upon their weak little intellects.

"Why, men fought before and always have fought, and nothing of the sort happened. Strife is a law of nature," they say with conviction and calmness, growing pale, nevertheless, seeking for the doctor with their eyes, and calling out hurriedly: "Water, quick, a glass of water!"

They would willingly become idiots, those people, only not to feel their intellect reeling and their reason succumbing in the hopeless combat with insanity.

In those days, when men over there were constantly being turned into corpses, I could find no peace, and sought the society of my fellow-men; and I heard many conversations and saw many false smiling faces, that asserted that the war was far off and in no way concerned them. But much oftener I met naked, frank horror, hopeless, bitter tears and frenzied cries of despair, when the great Mind itself cried out of man its last prayer, its last curse, with all the intensity of its power:

"Whenever will the senseless carnage end?"

At the home of some friends, whom I had not seen for a long time, perhaps several years, I unexpectedly met a mad officer, invalided from the war. He was a school fellow of mine, but I did not recognise him: if he had lain for a year in his grave, he would have returned more like himself than he was then. His hair was grey and his face quite white, his features were but little changed—but he was always silent, and seemed to be listening to something, and this stamped upon his face a look of such formidable remoteness, such indifference to all around him, that it was fearful to talk to him. His relatives were told he went mad in the following circumstances: they were in the reserve, while the neighboring regiment was ordered to make a bayonet charge. The men rushed shouting "Hurrah" so loudly as almost to drown the noise of the cannon—and suddenly the guns ceased firing, the "Hurrah" ceased also, and a sepulchral stillness ensued: they had run up to the enemy and were charging him with their bayonets. And his reason succumbed to that stillness.

Now he is calm when people make a noise around him, talk and shout, he listens and waits; but if only there is a moment's silence, he catches hold of his head, rushes up to the wall or against the furniture, and falls down in a fit resembling epilepsy. He has many relations, and they take turns and surround him with sound, but there remain the nights, long solitary nights—but here his father, a grey-haired old man, slightly wandering in his mind too, helped. He hung the walls of his son's room with loudly ticking clocks, that constantly struck the hour at different times, and at present he is arranging a wheel, resembling an incessantly going rattle. None of them lose hope that he will recover, as he is only twenty-seven, and their house is even gay. He is dressed very cleanly—not in his uniform—great care is taken of his appearance, and he is even handsome with his white hair, young, thoughtful face and well-bred, slow, tired movements.

When I was told all, I went up and kissed his hand, his white, languid hand, which will never more be lifted for a blow—and this did not seem to surprise anybody very much. Only his young sister smiled at me with her eyes, and afterwards showed me such attention that it seemed as if I were her betrothed and she loved me more than anybody in the world. She showed me such attention that I very nearly told her about my dark empty rooms, in which I am worse than alone—miserable heart, that never loses hope. . . . And she managed it so that we remained alone.

"How pale you are and what dark rings you have under your eyes," she said kindly. "Are you ill? Are you grieving for your brother?"

"I am grieving for everybody. And I do not feel well."

"I know why you kissed my brother's hand. They did not understand. Because he is mad, yes?"

"Yes, because he is mad."

She grew thoughtful and looked very much like her brother, only younger.

"And will you," she stopped and blushed, but did not lower her eyes, "will you let me kiss your hand?"

I kneeled before her and said: "Bless me."

She paled slightly, drew back and whispered with her lips:

"I do not believe."

"And I also."

For an instant her hand touched my head, and the instant was gone.

"Do you know," she said, "I am leaving for the war?"

"Go! But you will not be able to bear it."

"I do not know. But they need help, the same as you or my brother. It is not their fault. Will you remember me?"

"Yes. And you?"

"And I will remember you too. Good-bye!"

"Good-bye for ever!"

And I grew calm and felt happier, as if I had passed through the most terrible that there is in death and madness. And yesterday, for the first time, I entered my house calmly without any fear, and opened my brother's study and sat for a long time at his table. And when in the night I suddenly awoke as if from a push, and heard the scraping of the dry pen upon the paper, I was not frightened, but thought to myself, almost with a smile:

"Work on, brother, work on! Your pen is not dry, it is steeped in living human blood. Let your paper seem empty —in its ominous emptiness it is more eloquent of war and reason than all that is written by the most clever men. Work on, brother, work on!"

. . . And this morning I read that the battle is still raging, and again I was possessed with a dread fear and a feeling of something falling upon my brain. It is coming, it is here; it is already standing upon the threshold of these empty, light rooms. Remember, remember me, dear girl; I am going mad. Thirty thousand dead, thirty thousand dead! . . .

FRAGMENT XVII

. . . A FIGHT is going on in the town. There are dark and dreadful rumours. . . .

FRAGMENT XVIII

THIS morning, looking through the endless list of killed in the newspaper, I saw a familiar name; my sister's affianced husband, an officer called for military service at the same time as my dead brother, was killed. And, an hour later, the postman handed me a letter addressed to my brother, and I recognized the handwriting of the deceased on the envelope: the dead was writing to the dead. But still it was better so than the dead writing to the living. A mother was pointed out to me who kept receiving letters from her son for a whole month after she had read of his terrible death in the papers: he had been torn to pieces by a shell. He was a fond son, and each letter was full of endearing and encouraging words and youthful, naïve hopes of happiness. He was dead, but wrote of life with a fearful accuracy every day, and the mother ceased to believe in his death; and when a day passed without any letter, then a second and a third, and the endless silence of death ensued, she took a large old-fashioned revolver belonging to her son in both hands, and shot herself in the breast. I believe she survived, but I am not sure; I never heard.

I looked at the envelope for a long time, and thought:

He held it in his hands, he bought it somewhere, he gave the money to pay for it, and his servant went to fetch it from some shop; he sealed and perhaps posted it himself. Then the wheel of the complex machine called "post" came into action, and the letter glided past forest, fields and towns, passing from hand to hand, but rushing infallibly towards its destination. He put on his boots that last morning, while it went gliding on; he was killed, but it glided on; he was thrown into a pit and covered up with dead bodies and earth, while it still glided on past forests, fields and towns, a living phantom in a grey stamped envelope. And now I was holding it in my hands.

Here are the contents of the letter. It was written with a pencil on scraps of paper, and was not finished: something interfered.

". . . Only now do I understand the great joy of war, the ancient, primitive delight of killing man—clever, scheming, artful man, immeasurably more interesting than the most ravenous animal. To be ever taking life is as good as playing at lawn-tennis with planets and stars. Poor friend, what a pity you are not with us, but are constrained to weary away your time amidst an unleavened daily existence! In the atmosphere of death you would have found all that your restless, noble heart yearned for. A bloody feast—what truth there is in this somewhat hackneyed comparison! We go about up to our knees in blood, and this red wine, as my jolly men call it in jest, makes our heads swim. To drink the blood of one's enemy is not at all such a stupid custom as we think: they knew what they were doing. . . .

". . . The crows are cawing. Do you hear, the crows are cawing. From whence have they all gathered? The sky is black with them; they settle down beside us, having lost all fear, and follow us everywhere; and we are always underneath them, like under a black lace sunshade or a moving tree with black leaves. One of them approached quite close to my face and wanted to peck at it: he thought, most probably, that I was dead. The crows are cawing, and this troubles me a little. From whence have they all gathered? . . .

". . . Yesterday we stabbed them all sleeping. We approached stealthily, scarcely touching the ground with our feet, as if we were stalking wild ducks. We stole up to them so skilfully and cautiously that we did not touch a corpse and did not scare one single crow. We stole up like shadows, and the night hid us. I killed the sentry myself— knocked him down and strangled him with my hands, so as not to let him cry out. You understand: the slightest sound, and all would have been lost. But he did not cry out; he had no time, I believe, even to guess that he was being killed.

"They were all sleeping around the smouldering fires— sleeping peacefully, as if they were at home in their beds. We hacked about us for more than an hour, and only a few had time to awake before they received their death-blow. They howled, and of course begged for mercy. They used their teeth. One bit off a finger on my left hand,

with which I was incautiously holding his head. He bit off
my finger, but I twisted his head clean off: how do you
think—are we quits? How they did not all wake up I
cannot imagine. One could hear their bones crackling and
their bodies being hacked. Afterwards we stripped all
naked and divided their clothes amongst ourselves. My
friend, don't get angry over a joke. With your suscepti-
bility you will say this savours of marauding, but then we
are almost naked ourselves; our clothes are quite worn-out.
I have been wearing a woman's jacket for a long time, and
resemble more a . . . than an officer of a victorious army.
By the bye, you are, I believe, married, and it is not quite
right for you to read such things. But . . . you understand? Women. D—n it, I am young, and thirst for love!
Stop a minute: I believe it was you who was engaged to
be married? It was you, was it not, who showed me the por-
trait of a young girl and told me she was your promised
bride?—and there was something sad, something very sad
and mournful underneath it. And you cried. That was a
long time ago, and I remember it but confusedly; there is
no time for softness at war. And you cried. What did
you cry about? What was there written that was as sad
and mournful as a drooping flower? And you kept crying
and crying. . . . Were you not ashamed, an officer, to cry?

". . . The crows are cawing. Do you hear, friend, the
crows are cawing. What do they want?"

Further on the pencil-written lines were effaced and it
was impossible to decipher the signature. And strange to
say the dead man called forth no compassion in me. I dis-

tinctly pictured to myself his face, in which all was soft and delicate as a woman's: the color of his cheeks, the clearness and morning freshness of the eyes, the beard so bushy and soft, that a woman could almost have adorned herself with it. He liked books, flowers and music, feared all that was coarse, and wrote poetry—my brother, as a critic, declared that he wrote very good poetry. And I could not connect all that I knew and remembered of him with the cawing crows, bloody carnage and death.

. . . The crows are cawing. . . .

And suddenly for one mad, unutterably happy instant, I clearly saw that all was a lie and that there was no war. There were no killed, no corpses, there was no anguish of reeling, helpless thought. I was sleeping on my back and seeing a dream, as I used to in my childhood: the silent dread rooms, devastated by death and terror, and myself with a wild letter in my hand. My brother was living, and they were all sitting at the tea-table, and I could hear the noise of the crockery.

. . . The crows are cawing. . . .

No, it is but true. Unhappy earth, it is true. The crows are cawing. It is not the invention of an idle scribbler, aiming at cheap effects, or of a madman, who has lost his senses. The crows are cawing. Where is my brother? He was noble-hearted and gentle and wished no one evil. Where is he? I am asking you, you cursed murderers. I am asking you, you cursed murderers, crows sitting on carrion, wretched, imbecile animals, before the whole world. For you are animals. What did you kill my brother for?

If you had a face, I would give you a blow upon it, but you have no face, you have only the snout of a wild beast. You pretend that you are men, but I see claws under your gloves and the flat skull of an animal under your hat; hidden beneath your clever conversation I hear insanity rattling its rusty chains. And with all the power of my grief, my anguish and dishonored thought—I curse you, you wretched, imbecile animals!

FRAGMENT THE LAST

". . . WE look to you for the regeneration of human life!"

So shouted a speaker, holding on with difficulty to a small pillar, balancing himself with his arms, and waving a flag with a large inscription half-hidden in its folds: "Down with the war!"

"You, who are young, you, whose lives are only just beginning, save yourselves and the future generations from this horror, from this madness. It is unbearable, our eyes are drowned with blood. The sky is falling upon us, the earth is giving way under our feet. Kind people . . ."

The crowd was buzzing enigmatically and the voice of the speaker was drowned at times in the living threatening noise.

". . . Suppose I am mad, but I am speaking the truth. My father and brother are rotting over there like carrion. Make bonfires, dig pits and destroy, bury all your arms. Demolish all the barracks, and strip all the men of their bright clothes of madness, tear them off. One cannot bear it. . . . Men are dying . . ."

Somebody very tall gave him a blow and knocked him off the pillar; the flag rose once again and fell. I had no time to see the face of the man who struck him, as instantly everything turned into a nightmare. Everything became commotion, became agitated and howled; stones and logs of wood went flying through the air, fists, which were beating somebody, appeared above the heads. The crowd, like a living, roaring wave, lifted me up, carried me along several steps and threw me violently against a fence, then carried me back and away somewhere, and at last pressed me against a high pile of wood, that inclined forwards, threatening to fall down upon somebody's head. Something crackled and rattled against the beams in rapid dry succession; an instant's stillness—and again a roar burst forth, enormous, open-mouthed, terrible in its overwhelming power. And then the dry rapid crackling was heard again and somebody fell down near me with the blood flowing out of a red hole where his eye had been. And a heavy log of wood came whirling through the air and struck me in the face, and I fell down and began crawling, whither I knew not, amidst the trampling feet, and came to an open space. Then I climbed over some fences, breaking all my nails, clambered up piles of wood; one pile fell to pieces under me and I fell

amidst a cataract of thumping logs; at last I succeeded with
difficulty in getting out of a closed-in space—while behind
me all crashed, roared, howled and crackled, trying to over-
take me. A bell was ringing somewhere; something fell
with a thundering crash, as if it were a five-story house.
The twilight seemed to have stopped still, keeping back the
night, and the roar of shots, as if steeped in red, had
driven away the darkness. Jumping over the last fence I
found myself in a narrow, crooked lane resembling a corridor, between two obscure walls, and began running. I ran
for a long time, but the lane seemed to have no outlet; it
was terminated by a wall, behind which piles of wood and
scaffolding rose up black against the sky. And again I
climbed over the mobile, shifting piles, falling into pits,
where all was still and smelt of damp wood, getting out of
them again into the open, not daring to look back, for I
knew quite well what was happening by the dull reddish
color that tinged the black beams and made them look like
murdered giants. My smashed face had stopped bleeding
and felt numbed and strange, like a mask of plaster; and
the pain had almost quite disappeared. I believe I fainted
and lost consciousness in one of the black holes into which
I had fallen, but I am not certain whether I only imagined
it or was it really so, as I can remember myself only running.

I rushed about the unfamiliar streets, which had no lamps,
past the black death-like houses for a long time, unable to
find my way out of the dumb labyrinth. I ought to have
stopped and looked around me to define the necessary direc-

tion, but it was impossible to do so: the still distant din and howl was following at my heels and gradually overtaking me; sometimes, at a sudden turning, it struck me in the face, red and enveloped in clouds of livid, curling smoke, and then I turned back and rushed on until it was at my back once more. At one corner I saw a strip of light, that disappeared at my approach: it was a shop that was being hastily closed. I caught a glimpse of the counter and a barrel through a wide chink, but suddenly all became enveloped in a silent, crouching gloom. Not far from the shop I met a man, who was running towards me, and we almost collided in the darkness, stopping short at the distance of two steps from each other. I do not know who he was: I only saw the dark alert outline.

"Are you coming from over there?" he asked.

"Yes."

"And where are you running to?"

"Home."

"Ah! Home?"

He was silent for an instant and suddenly flung himself upon me, trying to bring me to the ground, and his cold fingers searched hungrily for my throat, but got entangled in my clothes. I bit his hand, loosened myself from his grip and set off running through the deserted streets with him after me, stamping loudly with his boots, for a long time. Then he stopped—I suppose the bite hurt him.

I do not know how I hit upon my street. It had no lamps either, and the houses had not a single light, as if they were dead, and I would have run past without recognising it, if

I had not by chance lifted my eyes and seen my house. But
I hesitated for some time: the house in which I had lived
for so many years seemed to me unfamiliar in that strange
dead street, in which my loud breathing awakened an extraordinary and mournful echo. Then I was seized with a
sudden wild terror at the thought that I had lost my key
when I fell, and I found it with difficulty, although it was
there all the time in the pocket of my coat. And when I
turned the lock the echo repeated the sound so loudly and
extraordinarily, as if all the doors of those dead houses in
the whole street had opened simultaneously.

. . . At first I hid myself in the cellar, but it was terrible
and dull down there, and something began darting before
my eyes, so I quietly stole into the rooms. Groping my
way in the dark, I locked all the doors and after a short
meditation decided to barricade them with the furniture, but
the sound of the furniture being moved was terribly loud
in the empty rooms and terrified me. "I shall await death
thus. It's all the same," I decided. There was some water,
very warm water in the water-jug, and I washed my face
in the dark and wiped it with a sheet. The parts that were
smashed galled and smarted much, and I felt a desire to
look at myself in the looking-glass. I lit a match—and in
its uneven, faint light there glanced at me from out of the
darkness something so hideous and terrible that I hastily
threw the match upon the floor. I believe my nose was
broken. "It makes no difference now," said I to myself.
"Nobody will mind."

And I felt gay. With strange grimaces and contortions

of the body, as if I were personating a thief on the stage, I
went into the larder and began searching for food. I
clearly saw the unsuitableness of all my grimaces, but it
pleased me so. And I ate with the same contortions, pre-
tending that I was very hungry.

But the darkness and quiet frightened me. I opened the
window into the yard and began listening. At first, probably as the traffic had ceased, all seemed to me to be quite
still. And I heard no shots. But soon I clearly distinguished
a distant din of voices: shouts, the crash of something falling, a laugh. The sounds grew louder perceptibly. I
looked at the sky; it was livid and sweeping past rapidly.
And the coach-house opposite me, and the paving of the
streets, and the dog's kennel, all were tinged with the same
reddish glare. I called the dog softly—

"Neptune!"

But nothing stirred in the kennel, and near it I distinguished in the livid light a shining piece of broken chain.
The distant cries and noise of something falling kept on
growing, and I shut the window.

"They are coming here!" I said to myself, and began
looking for some place to hide myself. I opened the stoves,
fumbled at the grate, opened the cupboards, but they would
not do. I made the round of all the rooms, excepting the
study, into which I did not want to look. I knew he was
sitting in his armchair at his table, heaped with books, and
this was unpleasant to me at that moment.

Gradually it began to appear that I was not alone: around
me people were silently moving about in the darkness. They

almost touched me, and once somebody's breath sent a cold
thrill through the back of my head.

"Who is there?" I asked in a whisper, but nobody answered.

And when I moved on they followed me, silent and terrible. I knew that it was only a hallucination because I was
ill and apparently feverish, but I could not conquer my fear,
from which I was trembling all over as if I had the ague. I
felt my head: it was hot as if on fire.

"I had better go there," said I to myself. "He is one of
my own people after all."

He was sitting in his armchair at the table, heaped with
books, and did not disappear as he did the last time, but
remained seated. The reddish light was making its way
through the red drawn curtains into the room, but did not
light up anything, and he was scarcely visible. I sat down
at a distance from him on the couch and waited. All was
still in the room, while from outside the even buzzing noise,
the crash of something falling and disjointed cries were
borne in upon us. And they were nearing us. The livid
light became brighter and brighter, and I could distinguish
him in his armchair—his black, iron-like profile, outlined
by a narrow stripe of red.

"Brother!" I said.

But he kept silence, immobile and black, like a monu-
ment. A board cracked in the next room and suddenly all
became so extraordinarily still, as it is where there are many
dead. All the sounds died away and the livid light itself
assumed a scarcely perceptible shade of deathliness and

stillness and became motionless and a little dim. I thought the stillness was coming from my brother and told him so.

"No, it is not from me," he answered. "Look out of the window."

I pulled the curtains aside and staggered back.

"So that's what it is!" said I.

"Call my wife; she has not seen that yet," ordered my brother.

She was sitting in the dining-room sewing something and, seeing my face, rose obediently, stuck her needle into her work and followed me. I pulled back the curtains from all the windows and the livid light flowed in through the broad openings unhindered, but somehow did not make the room any lighter: it was just as dark and only the big red squares of the windows burned brightly.

We went up to the window. Before the house there stretched an even, fiery red sky, without a single cloud, star or sun, and ended at the horizon, while below it lay just such an even dark red field, and it was covered with dead bodies. All the corpses were naked and lay with their legs towards us, so that we could only see their feet and triangular heads. And all was still; apparently they were all dead, and there were no wounded left behind in that endless field.

"Their number is growing," said my brother.

He was standing at the window also, and all were there: my mother, sister and everybody that lived in the house. I could not distinguish their faces, and could recognise them only by their voices.

"It only seems so," said my sister.

"No, it's true. Just look."

And, truly, there seemed to be more bodies. We looked attentively for the reason and found it: at the side of a corpse, where there was a free space, a fresh corpse suddenly appeared; apparently the earth was throwing them up. And all the unoccupied spaces filled rapidly, and the earth grew lighter from the light pink bodies, that were lying side by side with their feet towards us. And the room grew lighter, filled with a light pink dead light.

"Look, there is not enough room for them," said my brother.

And my mother answered:

"There is one here already."

We looked round: behind us on the floor lay a naked, light pink body with its head thrown back. And instantly at its side there appeared a second, and a third. And the earth threw them up one after the other, and soon the orderly rows of light pink dead bodies filled all the rooms.

"They are in the nursery too," said the nurse. "I saw them."

"We must go away," said my sister.

"But we cannot pass," said my brother.

"Look!"

And sure enough, they were lying close together, arm to arm, and their naked feet were touching us. And suddenly they stirred and swayed and rose up in the same orderly rows: the earth was throwing up new bodies, and they were lifting the first ones upwards.

"They will smother us!" said I. "Let us save ourselves through the window."

"We cannot!" cried my brother. "We cannot! Look what is there!"

. . . Behind the window, in a livid, motionless light stood the Red Laugh.

THE END